Paul Cela

ALSO BY YOKO TAWADA
from New Directions

The Bridegroom Was a Dog
The Emissary
Facing the Bridge
Memoirs of a Polar Bear
The Naked Eye
Scattered All Over the Earth
Three Streets
Where Europe Begins

Yoko Tawada

Paul Celan & the Trans-Tibetan Angel

translated from the German
by Susan Bernofsky

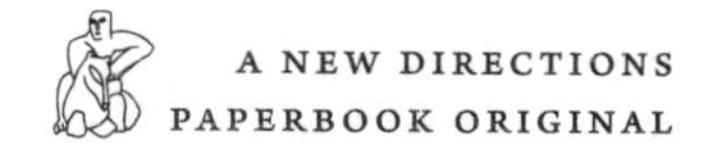
A NEW DIRECTIONS
PAPERBOOK ORIGINAL

Originally published as *Paul Celan und der chinesische Engel* by Konkursbuch Verlag, Tübingen, Germany.

An excerpt from this translation first appeared in *Granta 165: Deutschland.*

First published as New Directions Paperbook 1605 in 2024
Manufactured in the United States of America
Design by Erik Rieselbach

Library of Congress Cataloging-in-Publication Data
Names: Tawada, Yōko, 1960– author. | Bernofsky, Susan, translator.
Title: Paul Celan and the trans-Tibetan angel / Yoko Tawada ;
translated from the German by Susan Bernofsky.
Other titles: Paul Celan und der chinesische Engel. English
Description: New York, NY : New Directions Publishing Corporation, 2024.
Identifiers: LCCN 2024009109 | ISBN 9780811234870 (paperback) |
ISBN 9780811234887 (ebook)
Subjects: LCSH: Friendship—Fiction. | Diseases—Fiction. | LCGFT: Novels.
Classification: LCC PT2682.A87 P3813 2024 | DDC 833/.92—dc23/eng/20240227
LC record available at https://lccn.loc.gov/2024009109

10 9 8 7 6 5 4 3 2 1

New Directions Books are published for James Laughlin
by New Directions Publishing Corporation
80 Eighth Avenue, New York 10011

Paul Celan and the Trans-Tibetan Angel

1. *Singable Growth*

At every intersection, the patient regrets not carrying dice in his pocket to decide for him whether to keep going in the same direction or turn. Going straight means crossing the next street. Should he ignore the red light or wait for green? Obediently waiting for the light to change would be too square, and ignoring the color of blood too risky. And what if the light just happens to turn green as he approaches? That wouldn't solve anything either. There's no such thing as chance, and even if there is, the dice are loaded.

Green is out of the question, so is red. His only hope is the yellow light, a neutral in-between zone. The quince-yellow eye blinks open for two seconds and then shuts again. To seize this opportunity, he'd have to turn into a panther. The patient—not a panther—should forget all about trying to zip down the crosswalk's zebra back, and instead hang a quick left. Luckily he's walking on the left side of the street, and not by chance: he always turns left when he leaves the house, no matter whether the building in question is his own or the one where his girlfriend lives.

If he turned right at this juncture, he'd soon arrive

at a tiny supermarket where one of the cashiers always scowls and the other has compassionate eyes. To which of them will he hand over his money? Walking into a supermarket is Russian roulette.

Since he turns left, a café soon appears. In passing he glances at the coffee drinkers, harvesting their faces like golden grains of wheat. A forehead strikes his eye, a clever forehead belonging to a woman. The patient finds himself ever shorter of breath; the whites of his eyes gleam. Her silver necklace glitters like the Milky Way, and her lips converse without respite. Across from her sits a second woman with a similar hairstyle. Suddenly the woman's mouth falls silent. How marvelous, that instant when silence enters and the lips part ever so slightly, this time without a voice, as though she were about to kiss him. For the moment, no kissing occurs. First the screenplay has to be written. The patient, who finds traditional words ugly, isn't able to write. The word *kissing*, for example, tastes like dill pickle salad. *Nocturnal tonguejests* would work as an alternate expression. But to use it would be plagiarism.

As the patient zeroes in on the stranger's lips, his gaze becomes more critical, colder. There's something wrong with them. Lying there horizontally, the lips resemble two dead pieces of meat, producing a structural error: one lip lies atop the other as if it wished to be labeled *upper lip*. Every sort of hierarchy makes the patient sad. Really the lips should stand vertically on end and enjoy equal rights. While he's busy overthinking this, something happens that he fears most of all: the absolutely ideal lips appear before him. They possess neither shape nor color. They are perfect but dead. The patient coughs vigorously into his elbow, half-covering his face. Then he lets his arm drop, gives a shy smile, and cedes his place in line to the next passerby: I'm in no particular need, no really, do go ahead, I'm perfectly fine without a kiss. To be honest, I'm incapable of enduring intense physical contact right now. Please, be my guest, enjoy everything on offer here. I'm sure you'll be a worthy replacement for me.

The patient is surprised to see it's not a man but a woman standing behind him ready to step in and take his place. Women are just better at certain things, and there's nothing objectionable about having a woman fill in for you. To be honest, he doesn't even think it's the trouser-role tradition coming into play here—it's just that he put on trousers by accident this morning. He needs to take them off, and since he can't go to work without them, he might as well stay in bed. Getting sick is one thing, acquiring a doctor's note quite another. The doctor clicks words on his screen. Tiredness, listlessness, loss of appetite, inability to concentrate, insomnia: made-up words, every single one! The patient knows that not only these words but all the others, too, are inventions—they didn't grow naturally in the soil.

In any case, he definitely needs a replacement. His stingy institute is only willing to fund a half-time position, in other words, to pay for half an academic. Half a person can't stay healthy. The person's other half—the unemployed half—gets sick too. Both together take up a full two hours in the doctor's schedule. At the institute, the work requires a replacement with two hands. So in the end it's a matter of two people, not half a person. Why didn't the institute just create two positions right from the start?

The patient reaches out to shake his replacement's hand, but there's no longer a woman anywhere to be seen, and his hand floats aimlessly in midair. That's odd. She was just standing there right behind me. Maybe she got cold feet. Who's going to push open the double-winged doors in my place now?

The patient discovers a beautifully tailored figure off in the distance: a comet-like lady coming from the direction from which he, too, arrived. He feels ashamed. His faded shirt, missing buttons, wallet containing only coins. This lady is the flower of all flowers. The scent of chamomile flies up his nose, piercing his brain. The patient feels the urge to sink to his knees because the lady before him is a prima donna who sings the lead in every production; she's a diva but still as modest as an ornithologist. Each of her footsteps lands precisely on the beat, but there's nothing staccato about her way of walking; she moves in elegantly elongated, uninterrupted inhalations. With this gentle, decisive gait, she swiftly passes through the double winged door.

The patient feels proud. Except for him, no one knows that this opera singer lives in Berlin and not the US, as most music fans believe. She even lives in his neighborhood—somewhere off to the right, or else she wouldn't always be following in his footsteps.

He always turns left when he leaves the house, but he hardly ever leaves the house, since he hardly ever gets out of bed, and so he hardly ever has occasion to turn left. He can't remember the last time he left his pillow. When the doctor asks, he tells him he takes a walk every morning. He says this to please the doctor but, oddly, the lab coat recommends staying indoors, particularly in the case of persons incapable of recognizing an invisible danger. Anything else would be foolhardy. But the patient can spot danger more quickly than an emotionally stable individual. Despite the medical warning, he goes outside. Every morning or never: he's not quite sure.

On the left, his heart beats in his chest at an accelerated rate; on the right, day draws to a close with the purchase of a carton of milk at the supermarket. Without milk, the coffee tastes burned to him. With coffee, the milk tastes burned. The milk he buys is only 3.5% maternal. The rest is paternal. It tastes watery, a bit salty. He can't get anyone to tell him where he can buy thicker milk.

There's no wall blocking the path in any direction, so a person can go where they want. But when it comes right down to it, there's really only a single direction: from backstage to front and center. The thick wall behind the stage is really just made of velvet. The curtain is heavy, but anyone can open it. The front of the stage is mercilessly illuminated: that's where the singer has to stand. Once she's crossed this threshold, there's no turning back, and no one—not even this veteran artist—can maintain complete control over her vocal cords, because voices are not the exclusive property of humankind. When a person's voice abandons them, no one can help, not even the artificial heavens overhead, embroidered with golden stars. The musicians, who are bowing, banging, or blowing, fill up every last bit of space with sound, only to produce an enormous silence a moment later—a silence that she, the prima donna, must break all by herself with her opening note. There's always a song to sing, but first a silence must be created for the song to be born in.

The voice doesn't come from her mouth. It begins somewhere else, high up in the air where an invisible angel waves to her. No one in the audience can pinpoint the sound's location.

The patient stares at the double-winged door through which the singer vanished. The door is the plastic case of the DVD. He observes the women visiting the café. It's said that half of all human beings are women. But that can't be right. They are definitely more than half. Otherwise the system would collapse. Everywhere he looks, he sees more women than men. Women displaying their skin to the sun. Gleaming upper arms, napes sprinkled with freckles, and a V-shape between their covered breasts. There are also women who toss their luxuriant heads of hair over their shoulders and bring their faces closer and closer to his. He retreats, taking many tiny steps, so as not to be overwhelmed. His feet can already feel the sidewalk's edge. If he retreats just one step more, he'll fall off the curb.

Only members of the bourgeoisie are allowed inside concert halls. The patient wishes he were bourgeois, although secretly he believes the bourgeoisie are no better than the general populace, just somewhat more arrogant. Even after the singer goes to all that extra trouble to sing in Italian, they thank her by voting for the populists, or, as the patient likes to call them, *poplarists*. Writing *poplar* is a way of getting around the word *people*. The humble, hard-working diva studies the Russian libretto before she sings—and then her public opts for the autocrat. The patient shuts his eyes, wanting to be alone. He'd rather sit in an empty auditorium. Among other things, empty means filled with the dead. The concert hall officially counts as empty because the dead don't purchase tickets. They show up in a statistic but otherwise remain invisible, gathering wherever there's music to be heard. The patient thinks he might have to be dead himself to attend. He likes the idea of being dead, or even better: becoming dead. How does one become dead? It's not the same as dying. Merrily dead and always in attendance.

At this point he strokes his forehead with three fingers. This calms him. He doesn't want to think too much, he wants to walk. Walking is a way of thinking without words. He has difficulty clearing the word-foam from his head. His head isn't a space, it's a dense mass of unconnected words. Not only his brain but even the little hairs in his eyebrows and eyelashes are made of words. His stomach is full of words he finds he cannot digest. This morning for breakfast he ate the word *bread*. Yesterday, or the day before, or maybe some other day in the past, he bought a loaf of white bread at the supermarket. He urgently needed milk, so he went around the corner three times, making one left turn after the other. Eventually he arrived at the supermarket, where *bread* rhymes with *dead*.

Slice is a lovely word; it sounds like something stitched out of silk. A slice of bread. It sounds like warm flesh, a woman's torso draped in a silky scarf. Not the whole woman, just a thin slice of her. Even if the milk tastes burned, there's still a slice of hope in the bread. The patient thinks he's just eating words. In reality, he digests everything that goes along with them, too. Apparently, he swallowed the bread along with the word *bread* because he was hungry as usual, even though he didn't have an appetite.

He observes the beautiful singer at the same time every day. It amuses him that she seems not to realize he knows who she is. She thinks no one can recognize her because she's wearing a classic hat, big sunglasses, and a wide scarf that covers her mouth. She doesn't know that the patient recognizes people by their fingers, not their faces. In the past, he stood in the last row of the top balcony, and the singer on stage was as tiny as a thimble. He couldn't make out her individual fingers. Now that the concert halls have closed, the patient always sits in the front row at home. The stage has never been closer. When he goes to bed alone after visiting a digital performance space and sleeps through the night without closing his eyelids, a bright new dawn awaits him. There used to be so many gray-on-gray days. Now the sun brings its cheer and chastisement to all the days, and the city looks two-dimensional. To go on thinking in 3D, the patient must add his own shading to its contours.

Meanwhile all the opera houses are open again. At least that's what people are saying. But the patient has forgotten how to use any form of transportation. He doesn't remember how to stand on the platform in such a way that no crazy person can push him onto the tracks. Even the steps leading down to the platform are problematic. Walking down them reminds him of the descent into hell; walking up them, of the guillotine.

He should get out of the house. That would be a good first step. As a citizen, he has the right to leave reality behind at any moment. Standing on the sidewalk, he can be certain the singer will come from the right. If he turned right, the encounter would be over in a flash. He turns left, and the celebrity follows at his heels. He's afraid that she—not being afraid—will go on walking straight ahead, while he, unable to cross the street, has no choice but to turn to the left. To his astonishment, she turns left and enters the café. Its interior must be cool, dark, pleasant. But no one dares to go inside. No one wants to get so much sun. Those who've lost their homes are subjected to sunlight all day long. For those who can afford the price of some refreshing shade, sitting in an outdoor café is more or less an alibi. The winter will not come in which humankind will have the leisure to process this bizarre summer and come to terms with it. Spring won't come because winter isn't coming.

There used to be something called an intermission between acts. The curtain is pulled shut and the audience can no longer see anything onstage. The patient was insulted. How could the singer inflict this blindness on him? With his head bowed, he went out to the lobby and suddenly found himself in the middle of a crowd. Most of the people were well-dressed couples with silvery, wavy-stiff hair. Out of desperation, he went up to the counter and ordered a glass of sparkling wine whose acidity scratched at his insides. Everyone was standing elbow to elbow, making him feel all the more alone.

Fortunately, intermission-loneliness is a thing of the past. Intermissions have been outlawed nationwide. Recess at school is forbidden. No more taking a break in the asparagus field. The concert halls where one intermission after another used to be performed have shut their doors. All that's left are a few seconds of applause between two acts on a DVD, and without any intermission, the music starts back up again. The patient is enjoying his new front-row existence, this intermission-free life. He always hated recess as a child. During class, he could focus on his teacher and the pleasure she took in her quiet, talented pupil. Besides, there were textbooks to study, which gave him something to do. But during recess he had nothing to hold on to.

The patient exits the school building of his memory and approaches the large double-winged door. No door is ever closed to you if you feel strong enough, he thinks. But this double-winged door is a woman whom only a woman can open. The interior is a woman too. Of course, this woman isn't a matryoshka. Even if she were, I'm not the nutcracker who'll dance with her. I'll stay outside. That doesn't bother me. I don't like dolls anyhow, and little girls are puppets that stink of pee-pee. I've said this to my girlfriend on several occasions. I prefer a mature woman who's an artist in her own right and more famous than me. My girlfriend gives a contemptuous laugh and asks, Since when are you famous? Only two people know who you are: your mother and me. My girlfriend's face splits in half, revealing the face of my mother. Are all women just a single matryoshka? But how many times do I have to penetrate a woman's exterior before I can kiss a deeper layer?

Deep inside my skull, a dog starts barking its head off. It isn't just barking, there's also howling and neighing. Shh! I'm trying to sort out my thoughts! Every bark batters the fragile glass pane of his forehead. The patient kicks the animal a few times, making it bark even louder. Suddenly everything falls silent, and the patient understands that it's time for his entrance, but he doesn't know an aria to sing. Why did I attack the dog? It's my beloved dog Aorta. Haven't I often embraced him, shedding tears? And that one time I got drunk and reached for my paring knife, he playfully leapt into my lap, and I dropped the knife again. This Siberian husky trusted me completely even though his previous owner beat him and abandoned him in the woods. An American photographer who was out in the woods looking for particularly fine cedars found the dog and brought him to the SPCA. I read the ad in a local newspaper and went to get him. Right from the start, he ate everything right out of my hand: cookies, chips, autumn leaves. To this day I can feel his rough, hot tongue on the palm of my hand and between my fingers. My parents believed the dog's name was Franz. I never told them his real name. Aorta! This name, a personified secret, shall remain forever in my heart, even when I lie beneath the earth.

People say I'm sick because I can simultaneously

leave the house and stay home. Memory is its own house. Leaving it means going into a different house. It's not a contradiction to stay in one world while simultaneously leaving. He can make his entrance by withdrawing. He can be a patient and nonetheless remain a self.

The patient's name is Patrik. He sometimes refers to himself as the patient in his interior monologues. This is one of his survival strategies. Patrik's personal pronoun is *ich,* the first person (and therefore most important) in a unique singularity. Third person is a form of salvation, since it's unhealthy to always keep using that one good-natured little pronoun and conjugating all one's verbs accordingly: *ich habe, denke, esse, liebe, wasche, kaufe* (I have, think, eat, love, wash, buy), all with the little e-tail at the end. That's much too much monotony! No composer would allow his librettist to end all his lines with an *e.*

Patrik often feels confined in a first-person prison. The key that can free him from this cage lies in his hand. Unlocking the door isn't so easy for him. It hurts to stick that iron thing in the keyhole and twist it. A modern individual has to desire the opening. Opening hurts. Closing brings comfort.

The keyhole is his earhole. His ear bleeds an oily substance. Even though it hurts, sometimes it's better to be a patient than an *ich.* Otherwise he might stop getting any oxygen when he breathes. There are worse things than getting stabbed in the lung. If he gets stabbed several times in rapid succession, he'll run a fever. And if he's feverish, he won't have to go to the airport.

After Patrik registered for the Paul Celan conference in Paris, a query arrived from the organizers.

"What is your nationality?"

"Why do you ask?"

"Depending on your nationality, a different foundation might be responsible for covering the cost of your flight."

Patrik replies FRG, then regrets using the abbreviation. It's cowardly to speak only in capital letters. I'm an RA from the IFWLB and am traveling to the IPCC on AF: would that be an exemplary response? My sense of self-worth isn't elevated enough to let me speak in lowercase letters. Capital letters do offer some protection. Later he wrote to the organizers that he didn't wish to participate in this conference given the emphasis being placed on national origins.

I was born in Frankfurt, and every time I mention this, some know-it-all is quick to say: Oh, you must mean *Frankfurt an der Oder* on the Polish border! But the river I was born beside wasn't the Oder, it was the Main. The Main that runs through my Frankfurt is a tributary of the Rhine, which isn't

German property. But who's talking about ownership? I'm speaking of liquidity. I'm well aware that no foundation wants to chuck its money into running water. Stop! The patient doesn't want to think, he wants to walk. Walking is a rhythmical sort of thinking without commas. He completely forgets that his name is Patrik and walks fluently on his legs, which don't require names of their own. Legs are legs. Today's task is to leave the house and walk 10,000 steps. Leaving home is easy enough, particularly for a person who has already left their parents' home to start their own life. At first, life is found on the naked street. It's better to turn left. Patrik has a younger brother who also left his parents' house at the age of eighteen. His orientation, however, was to the right. He found it embarrassing that his big brother wore his hair long and sat in a café reading books written for girls. The patient can't remember if he really spent so much time at the café. He isn't even sure he has a right-wing brother. He's quite well-acquainted with his own inner lips being excellent liars. They lie whenever the opportunity presents itself. They lie day and night. They lie indefatigably for no reason at all, or for a reason unknown to him. What good is it to him to have a brother who's an active member of a populist or, to employ his own homemade concept, *poplarist* party? Well, yes, there is one way it's of use.

It definitely helps him to have a fake brother. This brother is a sort of landmark and helps him get his bearings. The patient lacks an inner compass. Telling well-calibrated lies is the only way he s draw a map in his head. Lying is useful. Still, it's no virtue to invent one's own facts. The patient suffers from a bad conscience. But he does have one consolation: he tells his lies without using his voice, and so this bad habit causes no harm to anyone around him.

His outer lips are honest and loyal. He never lies to his girlfriend. He tells her everything, including that he's fallen in love with that singer, whom he finds more mature and well-adjusted than her. His girlfriend's eyes flash with fire. Fingers trembling, she flings a ripe fig. The fruit has a cloying odor and silken skin. If the patient bites into it, the fruit's juicy red insides will appear: veins, fibers, flesh. Is he afraid? Patrik tastes blood on his tongue. His left cheek burns, the eardrum deafened. Was the fig perhaps a fist? Did his girlfriend scream? These events are now far away from him.

His girlfriend must have called him a long-haired loser obsessed with dead genres. What are dead genres? Poetry? Opera? Love? What were the actual words that left her lips instead of these? The original sentences have been lost and can no longer be reproduced here. The patient kept only his own translation, as is often the case in life.

Her boyfriend is a weakling who sits in a café reading sickly sweet lines of verse. And what should he be doing instead? Starting a business? Not exactly. All he has to do to satisfy his girlfriend is systematically select relevant poems, interpret them incisively, and land an academic position on the basis of this work. Of course, it'll have to be an interpretation you can't poke holes in. He'll have to submit to several needle stabs without screaming.

The girlfriend thinks: how can a weakling pass a qualifying examination? But she's forgotten the most important thing. The patient already has a position, a quite desirable one in fact. He sighs in relief. It was all just a nightmare. After he wakes up, he holds a long-term position as a research associate at a reputable institute. A few seconds later, though, he's no longer certain if he accepted this job or heroically turned it down. His employer pathologized Paul Celan, besmirched Ingeborg Bachmann, trivialized Nelly Sachs, and insulted various other noteworthy poets as if this were his calling. How can I accept such a person as my boss?

My inner lips are back to lying. No one's offered me a job. No one invited me to interview. How could I have turned down an offer? But it isn't true that no one's ever invited me. There was someone once who wanted to hire me: a jackdaw. One morning she asked if I wouldn't like to audition for her as a singer. A large quantity of blood rushed to my head, and my heart pounded against my breast from within, because the thought of auditioning filled me with great fear and intense desire. I imagined playing the role of Octavian in *Der Rosenkavalier*, singing his sentences while kneeling before the Marschallin. No, that isn't possible, because Octavian is written for a female voice. What does my future look like if the man I wish to be is only ever played by a woman?

Scholarship is too ascetic for me. I prefer a not-yet-knowing or a no-longer-knowing to actual knowledge. These are the fields in which I'll find my role. The patient never had any intention of walking a straight path. His girlfriend thought he was the sort of milksop that sits in a café reading poems, because what other sort of man would wear his hair long nowadays? That's gone out of fashion at least three times now. Does the patient really have long hair? Both his ears are visible, nakedly protruding. There's something bivalve-like and feminine about them. I'll slice them off and return them to my mother. Vincent van Gogh cut off an ear and gave it to a prostitute. With this act, the painter achieved his goal. He didn't want to be a leper locked in a bamboo cage. His illness is highly regarded, almost a crowning glory for an artist. The patient has short hair and undamaged ears. Some time ago he shaved his head. The words that had settled in his hair were too much for him. Tibetan monks shave their heads because their hair is constantly thinking about naked women. Does hair think? Certainly. More than the brain does. It was a spontaneous act: the patient first cut off all the hair he could grab with a pair of office scissors without looking in the mirror. He didn't have a mirror in his apartment. Then he shaved off the rest of the hair with a razor blade that injured his scalp in several spots. His girlfriend screamed like an emergency brake when she saw him.

"What have you done to your head? I don't want to be with a prisoner from a concentration camp!"

That's when he discovered she wanted to be with his hair, not with him. He took the hair out of the wastepaper basket, put it in an envelope, and mailed it to her with the commentary: "Here's your love back!" One might call this sentence harsh. Her asking what he'd done to his head was harsher still. She knows perfectly well what pain this sentence would cause him. He's been thinking for years about what was done to his head during his childhood. There must have been more to it than the innocent shaving of a juvenile skull.

The patient wishes to be a soft young man who wears his hair long and reads poetry. It's fine if his name is Patrik. As a patient he has more freedom, at least as long as his illness isn't named. Under his legal name, Patrik is required to undergo treatment. So how about letting this Patrik play a man who has already recovered? Maybe he hasn't begun his career yet, but that doesn't count as an illness. He's still young. He can enter the darkroom of poetry and gingerly touch his future with a fingertip. There are so many poetic professions in this world. It would be a miracle if he doesn't wind up in one of them. Poetry can be interpreted, discussed, presented, taught, reviewed, edited, published, sold, set to music, recited, staged, or translated, and if none of that works, he can still just become a poet. Most professions have died out in recent years, just like some of the incredibly beautiful insects of the Amazon.

Reading: that's the first step, regardless of what a person wishes to do professionally. Poetry: a good choice. Besides, Patrik looks quite handsome when he reads. His lashes grow longer, his lips redder. Nothing distracts him, not even the loud conversation at the next table. Right beside him, two women are passionately discussing liability insurance. They speak so openly that spit sprinkles down on their coffee cups like tropical rain. The patient is not yet

Patrik. The patient retraces his steps to the café and sits down next to the table where liability insurance is being discussed.

A minor time lag between the patient and Patrik shouldn't bother anyone. The patient notices that the bottoms of the table legs are rusted. For a stage set designer, this detail wouldn't be meaningless. Patrik is different from the patient. Patrik can forget about a defect like rust or mold that poses no immediate danger. Patrik calmly sits down and is perfectly capable of enduring a few seconds of heightened attention on the part of the other guests, something the patient would find challenging. The curiosity of city dwellers is short-lived. Even if he only had a single ear left like the Dutch painter, they wouldn't stare for long.

A waitress with close-cropped hair is just disappearing into the café's interior. She comes back out with a tray, sets two glasses of cola on the corner table, and goes back inside without noticing the new guest, Patrik. It's better to be invisible than disapproved of. Besides, I'm not here to drink, I'm here to read or, more precisely, to become a poetry-reading Patrik.

Instead of the waitress, the soprano appears and discovers a young man reading poetry. She wears a black dress and a long necklace made of large, delicate loops. Patrik knows this necklace. She sometimes wore it when she taught her master class. Now and then he watches videos in which the singer gives interviews. Of course, she isn't following a libretto when she does that. She alone decides what to wear, what to say, and how to move. The realization that the singer is leading a double life makes Patrik feel agitated. He's almost ready to accuse her of being a traitor.

Hugo von Hofmannsthal provided such elaborate stage directions it seems he wanted to control every last gesture of the future singers he would never meet. It's all there in black and white: when the Marschallin will sit up among her pillows, pull a curtain shut, or lie back down again. Reading the libretto fills Patrik with a sense of stubborn resistance, like a child whose mother is always telling him what to do. At the same time, he wishes a librettist would dictate the contents of his own life, which is otherwise empty. Patrik wants to be a character with a role to play. Hofmannsthal will forgive him if he adds a new character to the production. A young man completely absorbed in poetry who forgets the world around him. Other guests at the party are wearing price tags on their ears. This young man is unspoiled. Might he successfully court the *dame aux camellias*? No. He lacks the capacity to love or, more precisely, the capacity to sing. There are no vibrations between his windpipe and throat that transcend the merely mortal. He's an ordinary human being who suffers from shortness of breath. Alfredo, on the other hand, sings like a real tempest, transcending all humanity, a force of nature.

The patient finally notices the close-cropped waitress standing diagonally opposite him awaiting his response. Without knowing the question, he answers:

"Yes, I do."

"And what?" the waitress asks scornfully. A good question. What does he want? He's perfectly satisfied as is.

"You know, I'll take whatever you think appropriate. It's not always all about me."

Annoyed at this response, the waitress turns her back. Behind her shoulder blades, a pair of double-winged doors comes into view. Behind these doors, a lavish party is underway. You'd never guess, looking at the building's shabby exterior, that such an opulent marble fountain could be hidden within its walls. The fountain bubbles with champagne, and the glasses held aloft by the guests flash beneath the chandelier's rays. Hello, Paris! A courtesan shimmies from one gentleman to another, flirting in her five foreign tongues. The singer wears flowery clothes. The leaf-souls of the guests are blown back and forth by her hot breath. The singer's role is Violetta, a compassionate escort. All the champagne's been drunk and the guests move in pairs to the next room. Violetta is about to follow. Suddenly her chest convulses in a devilish coughing fit. She crouches down, making herself small, and slips into a dark sphere where no spotlight will ever find her. The guests are no longer nearby, except for one man, Alfredo, who clasps the coughing woman in his powerful arms. The patient breathes in syncopes. A voluntary faint lasting several seconds.

2. *The Texture of Angel-Matter*

The man standing in front of Patrik looks very *Trans-Tibetan*. This is the first time Patrik has ever used this Celan word, which he's been warming beneath his feathers for a long time now without knowing what group of people or languages would hatch from it. The man really does look Trans-Tibetan; this is a subjective impression, and the purpose of adjectives is to support subjectivity.

The man asks permission to join Patrik at his table. The language he speaks is no rara avis requiring a recherché description like Trans-Himalayan or Sino-Tibetan. He speaks a straightforward German with a faint accent. Other tables are occupied, and it's only logical, it seems to Patrik, for two men to share a table in solidarity.

"My name is Leo-Eric Fu," the man says, elegantly extending his hand and then quickly withdrawing it before Patrik can respond. Patrik understands that a greeting need not be physically consummated. There's a question buzzing circles in his head. Should a person reveal their full name right at the outset when making a fleeting café acquaintance, or are all three components—Leo, Eric, and Fu—his first names? Patrik is cautious and offers only the first of his given names.

"My name is Patrik."

"I know," Leo-Eric answers with an understanding nod. Patrik is unnerved, uncertain how to interpret this reply. Leo-Eric then says he's often observed Patrik sitting in this café—the last time, in fact, reading the book of poems *Fadensonnen* (*Thread suns*). Patrik has no memory of this, but it's certainly possible he was reading poetry at the café, especially since he was planning to give a paper at a Paul Celan conference in Paris. At the moment, he isn't sure if he'll be cleared to participate or if he'll be struck from the list of speakers as an oversensitive crackpot.

"You intend to give a talk on the book *Threadsuns*?"

"It's possible I intended to a few weeks ago. But now, no."

"Why not?"

Patrik can't find an answer to this question, so he quickly invents a reason, looking down.

"I don't like conferences."

"Why not?"

"I find it a stressful situation to be observed from all sides. All the people suddenly wearing devil's masks."

"What do you mean? I don't follow."

"First the talk, then questions, answers, discussion: it's like a play at the theater."

"Society *is* a theater, it seems to me. Democracy requires a backstory, a narrative structure, and well-rehearsed variations. You can't build a democracy on authentic feelings alone."

Patrik looks up again, wondering if this Leo-Eric isn't a freedom fighter from Hong Kong. One moment later, he erases this spontaneous conjecture from his brain-page. Someone from Beijing can be a freedom fighter, too. Patrik himself is the one least likely to be democracy-minded.

"I don't like questions, criticism, or discussion," Patrik responds. "But you can't say that out loud, and when it comes right down to it, I don't think it's all right that I am the way I am."

"What displeases you about discussion culture? Do explain, I'm genuinely curious."

A stormy chaos swirls up inside Patrik's head; it's a torment to be unable to sort out the multitude of multicolored thought-scraps. He invents a new theory, which at least gives him something to hold on to: Leo-Eric is collecting clips of people making antidemocratic statements. He's using a hidden microphone to record the authentic voices of EU citizens and selling them to countries where they'll be used as teaching material in language classes. Patrik taps three fingertips against the forehead behind which this absurd theory is taking shape. He's like a woodpecker hunting nice fat thought-worms in the bark to gobble up.

"I usually construct a conference paper as lovingly as you would build a sandcastle at the beach. I don't understand why most children are so cruel they want to destroy my sand art with their toy shovels."

Whenever Patrik hears the word *shovel,* he gets goose bumps. Now that he himself has uttered the word, he feels all crumpled up inside, but it consoles him when a smile appears at the corners of Leo-Eric's mouth as he says:

"Oh, the children don't mean anything by it. You shouldn't take their game so personally."

"If I don't take anything personally, what becomes of my person?"

"A toy shovel is as harmless as the little wooden spoon we eat ice cream with."

"Even a tiny medical spoon can grate on my nerves so brutally I can't stand it for even a second."

"An ice cream sundae with strawberries, please!"

This sentence isn't meant for Patrik. The waitress nods and places a cup of milk in front of him.

"Excuse me, I didn't order any milk."

"You left the decision to me. I think milk is the most suitable thing for you."

Patrik actually remembers what he said to her—at this moment he feels something like a continuity of time, which is rarely the case with him.

"Yes, that's right. I wanted to know what you think of me. I guess you think I still have my milk teeth?"

Haha, hilarious. Ignoring his words, the waitress turns to the next guest who has just lifted one hand in the air. Leo-Eric considers the Liquid Paper–white milk and says:

"You own a first edition of Paul Celan's *Threadsuns,* is that correct?"

This man appears to know even unimportant details about Patrik's life.

"I have the 1968 edition, but that's nothing special."

"Why not?"

"There are five thousand copies of it. I'm one of five thousand readers. A surprisingly large edition for a book that's so hard to understand. Even the Deutsche Oper only seats two thousand."

Leo-Eric emits a bright peal of laughter.

"Well, that doesn't mean five thousand people have actually read the book. Possibly you're one of only a very few still reading and thinking about this book today."

"I'm actually too tired to think about a complicated book. My girlfriend is the one who got it for me at a used bookstore as a birthday present. When she gave me the book, I was furious. I almost threw it in the garbage. But I found its snowy white dust jacket and slender body appealing, so I put it on the shelf anyway. A thicker book would have ended up in the fire."

"What did your girlfriend do wrong?"

"The absence of premeditation is paramount for me. Obviously, she wants to force me to write a talk. Every sort of well-meaning female manipulation is like snake venom."

Leo-Eric nods impassively and says: "A career can never be as radiant as a flame scallop."

Someone who isn't career-oriented can't possibly come from China, Patrik thinks. Maybe he's from Tibet. He's probably one of those monks that meditate day and night high up in the mountains without giving a thought to money or worldly careers. Patrik laughs inwardly and interrupts this train of clichéd thought by providing his own response: a Tibetan can also be a successful businessman and have an account at the Swiss Bank. Patrik doesn't want to go on speculating about where Leo-Eric comes from, instead he'll listen to his words. He just said a career isn't radiant like a flame scallop. This is a crystal-clear statement and worthy of a reply.

"If a career can't be a scallop, what can?"

Patrik has succeeded in asking a question that

moves the conversation along. After asking it, he goes on savoring the word *scallop* in his mouth like a sip of red wine. He uses dead words much too often to be understood, or else he reverts to the state of a patient who remains stubbornly silent in a therapy session. Now he can utter fresh-squeezed words without being accused of sickness. Leo-Eric inclines his head gently to the left, searching for a response. He takes his time.

When human beings fall silent, a music can be heard. A singer sings impatiently in a tree. She places her first note high, then lets her voice fall step by step before quickly ascending once again. A blackbird. You don't see her form until she comes down from her tree. Can so shy a singer sing at the top of her lungs? Oh yes, she's just the one to manage this. Exaggerated shyness is a sort of traffic jam. Behind the dam, the pressure builds until it's created enough electricity to power all the chandeliers in the concert hall. Patrik loses track of the blackbird and finds himself looking at Leo-Eric, who has something birdlike about him. Perhaps it's his slender neck or his eyes like black glass beads. Who's to say Leo-Eric isn't a blackbird? He watches people from high up in a tree, he collects facts, builds a nest of them, and, when he finds it useful, he appears in human form. There are people like Patrik who wait to receive help from winged beings. Finally Leo-Eric opens his mouth again.

"Do you know the No-Tree? It stands in the middle of an open field. You can ask it the same question from all eight points on the compass. The answer will be different every time, though it's always No."

To Patrik this sounds like a koan from the tradition of Zen Buddhism. Perhaps Leo-Eric comes from a country in which the most Zen Buddhists live today, in other words: France. This supposition is half-confirmed when Leo-Eric says:

"The word *career* comes from the French *carrière,* which also refers to a quarry. Perhaps this is why for some people a career seems as impenetrable as granite."

Patrik replies, "Everything about a career strikes me as highly disagreeable. I don't want to be trapped on a career path, I want to be free. No highway, no train tracks, I much prefer an open field without a footpath or trail. A free, modern human being must be able to walk in all directions. I don't just mean the four or eight points of the compass. There are more than eight directions."

"But the place where you grew up wasn't a central Asian steppe, it's a city full of high-rises."

"Yes, that's true."

"In a city, pedestrians and cars, for the most part,

can only move in four directions: backward, forward, left, and right. That's it. But four directions are already too much for you. To avoid the necessity of making a new decision at every moment, you've found a single answer that you apply to each situation."

"And what is this answer?"

"Turn left!"

Patrik swallows and blinks like a stroboscope. In the hectic alternation of light and shadow, his interlocutor vanishes. This makes it easier to speak.

"How do you know all that?"

"As I said, I've been observing you."

This beakless person cannot be a blackbird, Patrik thinks. Perhaps this intelligent-looking man comes from the northern half of the Korean peninsula and is wearing special contact lenses connected to a giant database. Patrik notices that his thinking has derailed again and considers how to get back to reality's main track. Leo-Eric knits his brows and says:

"Please don't be alarmed. I'm not a stalker."

A stalker! Patrik hadn't even thought of that. After all, the victim of a stalker is never a man in a wrinkled shirt with no color in his cheeks.

"No, I never suspected you of being a stalker, or more precisely: I can't imagine being the victim of such activity. I thought maybe a spy. But since I'm not in possession of any important information, this too is unthinkable. Or are you a Zen Buddhist spy who wants to steal the great Nothingness inside my head?"

Patrik has succeeded in joking his way out of an embarrassing situation. Leo-Eric laughs in relief and begins the fluent narration he's prepared:

"I came to speak with you about the channels that run through the human body. There are twelve main channels, which are called meridians. The word *meridian* comes from the French translation of the Chinese term *jingmai*."

Patrik responds reflexively:

"But there's only a single meridian. Why are you speaking of meridians in the plural?"

"Most people only consider a single meridian, the zero meridian, and suppress all the others."

"Well, after all, there aren't so many poetological texts by Paul Celan, so 'The Meridian' is really quite important to me."

"But can his poems be explained on the basis of just this one meridian?"

"Of course not. If a single meridian isn't enough for you, how many do you have to offer?"

"There are as many principal meridians as there are numbers on a clock: twelve."

"What are you talking about?"

"For example, the liver meridian begins in the big toe under the nail, crosses over the top of the foot and then goes up through the knee and thigh. It passes through the liver, the back of the throat, the nose, eyes, and forehead, until it reaches the crown of the head. If a person has a problem with their liver, you can use a needle to treat all the points that lie along this meridian."

"Aha, you're talking about acupuncture!"

Patrik feels infinitely relieved. Now he knows what's going on. But this breath-pause of relief doesn't last long. Leo-Eric draws him into a new vortex of confusion.

"No, I'm talking about a poem by Celan: 'DETOUR- / MAPS, phosphorus …' Do you know the poem?"

"Of course I do. This poem contains the word *aorta,* and as a child I had a dog named Aorta. In this respect, the poem also serves as a detour to my memory."

"A detour? When the liver isn't working right, we don't treat the liver itself, we treat the liver meridian. That's not a detour."

Patrik becomes aware of his big toes, which for some reason are having trouble sensing the ground beneath them.

"My feet are strangely present all at once. They can't find the ground."

"My grandfather used to say to me: pay attention to your own feet when you are speaking with someone! The foot is a nice thick book. Some people think only the eyes or heart are connected to the soul. That isn't true. The networks within the body are far more complex."

"But Celan couldn't have been talking about this sort of meridian. For him, only a single meridian existed."

"The meridian that passes through London? I don't believe that. For example, here's another meridian that was very important to Celan: the one connecting Paris with Stockholm."

Patrik remembers in a flash that a meridian appears in Celan's correspondence with Nelly Sachs. "Between Stockholm and Paris runs the meridian of pain and consolation," he quotes from memory and then says, "A number of meridians exist—metaphorically speaking. But I don't put any stock in metaphors, they're too spongy for me. I prefer to rely on numbers and letters for orientation."

Leo-Eric replies gently, "I'm speaking not metaphorically but geographically. Have you ever visited the historical observatory in Paris?"

"No."

"The so-called Paris meridian is found there, inlaid in the floor in multicolored stones."

"Didn't you say meridians are channels in the body?"

"What difference is there between the terrestrial sphere and the body? Place names and the names of organs were equally important as points of reference for the poet. We must search for the lines that connect them to one another."

"This is all very interesting," Patrik says. "Why don't you go to Paris for the conference yourself? You're the one who really should be giving a presentation on Celan and the meridian or, if you prefer, meridians."

"Unfortunately I can't do that. It isn't my area of expertise. My grandfather practiced traditional Chinese medicine in Paris in the 50s and 60s—the period when Celan was living there, too. My grandfather was a highly educated man who read Chinese, French, Hebrew, and German. In his papers after he died, I found the notes he'd made on Celan's poems."

"And then?"

"I can tell you some things that probably only a very few other people know. What you do with this information is your business. It's all the same to me whether you have success in your profession or not. What I have to offer isn't a career, it's just a handful of meridians."

3. *Woundable Fingers*

On his way home, the patient can no longer remember how he said goodbye to Leo-Eric. Apparently, they didn't shake hands when they parted, or he would feel a hint of warmth on his palm. There's a gap in his memory cinema. In the first scene, he sits at the café having an impassioned discussion with his new friend; in the next scene he's on his way home alone.

As he walks, he stares at the palm of his left hand as if it were the screen of a cell phone. No new messages. Still only the same old news: wrinkles and birthmarks. This hand is made of flesh just like a piece of meat on a platter, but supposedly it's made in the image of the hand of God—though it seems external resemblance isn't what is meant here. The foot, eye, and ear are also made in God's image. Who told me that? Certainly not Leo-Eric, he of the godless tongue. It was in a book about Kabbalah. Back when Patrik was still planning to prepare for the Celan conference in Paris, he checked out two shopping bags' worth of books from the Staatsbibliothek. Reading Gershom Scholem, he came across the title *Gates of Light* and felt a deep desire to pass through these gates himself. The author's name was Joseph—Patrik can't remember his last name at the moment. There was also a book about Kabbalah in which he found a very interesting table. Twelve letters were each assigned an organ: liver, gall bladder, kidney, and so forth, just like the principal meridians in traditional Chinese medicine. But what does Kabbalah have to do with acupuncture? Suddenly Patrik is seized with the desire to go back to the Staatsbibliothek. The palace of books has been fenced in and unapproachable for weeks. Now it's supposedly accessible again, but Patrik is afraid that if he goes there he'll find a massive abandoned construction site. The next time he sees Leo-Eric he wants to ask him if Celan ever came into contact with Chinese meridians in Paris. If not, that means the similarities between Kabbalah and Eastern medicine can be explained the same way as the resemblance between Patrik's hand and Leo-Eric's hand: they aren't genetically related but resemble one another all the same because they're both copies of the hand of God.

I've consciously been avoiding the word *God* ever since my brother began to abuse it. When we ran into each other by chance on the street in Berlin, he started talking about *God of the Storm, God of War, God of Death,* and I thought he meant a computer game. But these phrases actually originated from somewhere else, perhaps a Library of Hate. Why was this library still open when the Staatsbibliothek was closed? My brother spoke feverishly, driven on by a wind that struck him like a whip. He said something about how the hexagonal eyes must be destroyed. His rage was lukewarm, but the weapons stood ready to attack—he had only to activate them. At least, he claimed to possess bombs that he had made himself. I ran away from him without saying goodbye and ended up in a park full of climbing equipment plastered with colorful scrawls. My brother's words still swirled in my head: *fire, purgatory, burn, destroy*. Suddenly I realized he was trying to communicate something important to me. It was his intention to prevent an attack even as he was preparing for it. Didn't he tell me that he and his comrades were planning to set fire to the Temple of the Others? Did he utter the words "mosque" or "synagogue"? Neither. Nonetheless, it was clear he was talking about attempted destruction. I dragged my suddenly very heavy body to the old phone booth I had seen at the edge of the park and called the police. An officer answered the phone with a coffee-break voice. I told him a radicalized group was planning an arson attack at a mosque or synagogue. The officer's bass-baritone voice replied without emotion: "I don't doubt it." This answer was meant literally. I replaced the receiver, not wanting to reveal my brother's name.

Joseph ben Abraham Gikatilla! This is the name of the medieval author who wrote *Gates of Light*. In his opinion, man is incapable of grasping the essence of the Creator—not even an angel can, because an angel is bound to a single perspective. Only the Creator himself can grasp himself. How interesting that so unfathomably great a being as the Creator should possess a silly little body part like hands. Apparently, handiness isn't at odds with godliness.

The patient has a distanced relationship to his own hands. He would say he knows every letter in the word *hand*, but there's a missing piece that ought to unite the word and the hand itself. A soul could link the two together, but a soul is so old-fashioned, like sending a telegram. What appears to connect everything with everything nowadays isn't the soul—it's a digital network. The patient feels a strong affinity for the word *telegram*, as well as for the word *Tetragrammaton* that he learned from Gikatilla. This is the proper name of God. His profession is God, his name Tetragrammaton. Which personal pronoun he uses in the first person is something the patient doesn't know. He only knows that he is allowed to address him using the informal second-person pronoun *du*.

God must have a hand with no wrinkles since he

has no biography. The lines in the flesh of the palm—one line in particular—indicate the length of a life. The longer the lifeline, the farther away death is. The patient is disturbed by the fact that his lifeline veers off in the middle and vanishes at the base of his hand where three parallel creases look like a pictogram for *river*. The patient doesn't believe Celan jumped into the Seine voluntarily. While Celan looked down at the river's surface that night, someone pushed him into the water. This someone was a chance perpetrator. The patient wants to venture deep into the water to find the perp. Even chance must take some responsibility. The patient's legs are unsteady, he has astigmatism and doesn't wear glasses. There are various other reasons why the patient might fall in the water. No priest can stop him from spending time alone on the riverbank at night. He doesn't have a circle of friends to invite him to dinner. Only the arts and sciences, whose sturdy pillars support the heavy roof of the night sky, can possibly save him. Alas, there isn't any scholarly institute on this bank, where the unhoused spend the night in their sleeping bags, peering out through eye slits. For the most part, scholarly institutes are built on hilltops, far from water.

At the moment, the patient isn't looking for a pillar. A hand would suffice if it can hold him so he doesn't slip down any farther. Miracles do exist.

A hand reaches out to him as a bass-baritone voice suggests: "We have to talk! One on one." It sounds encouraging. Without the confusing voice that rises up from the chasm of history, he can now carry on a conversation. A conversation means two people. Each person has two eyes, for a total of four. The patient considers the four fingers of his own left hand. Each of them has an eye-shaped hinge. All four eyes close when he balls his fist up and they open again when he stretches out his fingers. We absolutely must speak one on one! The patient hears these words from his therapist, a self-proclaimed representative of the Tetragrammaton. *Tetra* stands for the number four: a perfect, perfectly self-contained number. This thought makes the patient uneasy. The number four has excluded the fifth participant for the sake of perfection. Shouldn't one speak five on five? Every hand has five eyes. Only a hand with five fingers can protect a person from the evil eye. With only four fingers, without the help of the thumb, the great apes would never have succeeded in making tools. The patient proposes including the fifth eye. The harried therapist asks the meaning of this request. One can see he's under twofold pressure: first because of general time pressure, and on top of that, he's under professional pressure to remain patient with his patient. Why do you believe we can't speak one on one? The patient can't answer this question because he doesn't want to draw attention to his thumb, which, aroused for no reason, is pointing up vertically like a pubic tower. A one-on-one conversation can easily go south, as the patient knows quite well from previous experience. Two people looking each other in the eye are two mirrors. An endless chain of confusions. The therapist's eyes become rectangular; his trembling lips are being used for speaking by some other person whom the patient doesn't know. Forget the five eyes! There are five Anglophone countries keeping a sharp eye on us and privately exchanging information. Five Eyes is an outrageous military surveillance system! The patient listens calmly, thinking to himself that the therapist must be suffering from delusions caused by the immoderate consumption of spy novels.

His desire to speak withers on the vine just as the hour covered by his health insurance comes to an end. The patient hastily exits the building complex, which bears the name CitizenHealth. The abruptly truncated conversation keeps turning over in his head like a printing press out of paper. There's a riotous hammering and clattering in this twilight hour that's too cowardly to pass into nocturnal silence. When God has lost his power, he should quickly leave the stage and not let twilight endlessly drag on. As if he were afraid of the dark! As if only bright daylight had any value and night were just an obligatory intermission full of scary dreams! Day is necessary, night is necessary, and passing from one to the other is a difficult art.

As soon as he's outside, he starts thinking of things he should have said back in the office. These unspoken words pursue him not only through the evening after a therapy session but for days and weeks thereafter. The patient goes on speaking with a hollow gaze. Walking down the street, he speaks like a person talking on the phone with a hidden microphone and a tiny button in his ear. Every path he takes turns into a long detour, making his way home resemble a carefree evening stroll.

The sun, using its last remaining strength, shoves the heavy curtain of clouds aside. The woman walking in front of the patient casts a long shadow from which a bat suddenly flies up, vanishing behind a rain gutter. Anyone who casts a shadow is human. The patient feels like a bat that couldn't manage to escape and now remains shackled to a laboratory table. The backs of its wings must be thoroughly investigated. The operating lamp is an enormous showerhead with five blinding eyes. The bat is yanked from the dark and subjected to cruel luminescence. It's said that songbirds generally bleed very little. A bat is a winged songmouse. Its song is an acquired taste possibly necessitating an acquired immunity. Its voice ascends far above the high C that even the most gifted soprano can reach only with effort. In this range, one no longer speaks of a voice but rather of ultrasound. A bat's voice can have a diabolical influence on an embryo if a pregnant woman happens to hear it. The newborn child will have long pointy ears and big round eyes. This is all just a murky legend. The bat playfully glides between its hunting shriek and an everyday conversational tone of voice. There's no struggle or strain to this up and down, it's not like plunging from the heights of infatuation to bitter disappointment—it's just a smooth, elegant line of flight. The bat's flight is just like its song. Its art is no secret, but no other living creature can achieve it. If you catch a bat and dissect it to analyze its abilities, you kill it. That doesn't matter, the researcher thinks, for the collection of microscopic life beneath the animal's wings is anything but hygienically correct and would shock the average citizen.

The therapist has meticulously well-groomed hands and won't so much as pick up a lucky ladybug without first donning rubber gloves. When the patient told him about certain Celan formulations like *your urine black* and *waterbilious your stool,* the therapist ducked into the back room, undoubtedly to disinfect his hands. If there could be no happiness without microbes, he would forego happiness. How can such a clean man touch me when I'm so dirty, the patient thinks. But he changes his opinion at once when he sees the therapist at an outdoor snack bar gripping a piece of Viennese sausage with his greasy-black fingernails. The therapist grins with gleaming lips and even gives him a wink, as if to say: a healthy man must consume hearty meat dishes, above all in Vienna. And indeed, this isn't Potsdamer Platz, it's Heldenplatz. The patient knows he's inside a dream. He hasn't been to Austria in years. The last time was Salzburg, where he saw a production of *The Woman without a Shadow* by Richard Strauss. And even though his favorite singer wasn't part of the performance, all the cells in his body synchronized with the music. For more than three hours, he sat as if shackled to his seat; it wasn't a pleasant experience but rather a fascinating sort of agony. Why is it necessary to compose the orchestral score in such a way that it not only doesn't support the singing but constantly undercuts it with little contrary impulses? Why do the words slip from the hands trying to grasp their meaning? Such disastrous music has no power to heal or even console. *There are / still songs to sing beyond / humankind.*

Eventually the patient began to find the very existence of Austria overwhelming. Too many musicians, too many composers, too many concerts: you're always missing everything if you don't travel there all the time. Actually living in Austria, on the other hand, is out of the question. It's too risky, especially in Vienna where so many streetcar lines terminate at Central Cemetery. He knows about that from reading Ilse Aichinger. Fortunately the patient no longer has to devote any more thought to the Habsburg territories. At some point the borders were closed and the old order returned. A Prussian remains in Prussia, a Romanov remains in Russia. Naturally, a Goethe or Mozart traveled across national borders, but a person like the patient needn't consider himself a loser just because he stays home. The Habsburgs aren't having such an easy time of it either; they can no longer expand their territories through arranged marriages now that kissing in general has been outlawed. The patient hasn't kissed anyone in a long time. Even when he's having a dream in which he knows he's dreaming, he can't steer the plot in an erotic direction. His unappetizing therapist talks on and on in the dream, and no one can make him stop. A person who can't digest lung meat, he says, will fall ill with consumption. In the case of a very thin man, this may even have fatal consequences, especially if he carries the shadow of tuberculosis around with him. Instead of the therapist, it's now an unknown practitioner copying the phrase *glottal stop* from the book of poems into a medical chart. A jackdaw that loses its voice will soon die. Kafka (the Czech word for jackdaw) abhorred Wien (the German word for Vienna). Never would he allow his sentences to sway to the three-quarter-time rhythm of the waltz. Celan didn't spend much time in the city of Johann Strauss either. The patient once—and really only a single time in his life—attended an intoxicating New Year's Eve celebration. At this party they played an oceanic waltz. His body began to sway so vigorously that he was hurled over the edge of the endurable. Crashing down on the concrete floor, he broke several bones. Never again, waltz! Does that even work?

The *W* of Wien comes not from the waltz but from Wittgenstein. Writing without the aroma of hearty dishes and sensually wobbling hip fat. Celan hated Vienna. Kafka hated Vienna. And so the patient, too, is allowed to hate this city. Secretly he loves it. He just doesn't want to dream of it too often.

While walking, the patient constantly churns out arguments to counter the voice of his adversary, who doesn't exist. It isn't the therapist. He realized that a long time ago. He just doesn't want to admit it. A battle against his own shadow. An autoimmune disorder of the mind. His last therapy session was a long time ago. The therapist took his own life and it wasn't possible to find out why. The patient called his health insurance and was told that the company was responsible only for health, not for death. The patient changed his strategy and asked about financing a new therapy. The woman handling this request replied apathetically that he would have to submit an application, adding with a sigh: *For the last time, psychology!* At this, the patient gave, for the first time, a friendly laugh, recognizing the line from a poem by Celan.

Health insurance thinks (if insurance can be said to think) that an illness like tuberculosis is outdated and fit for public consumption only—if at all—on the opera stage. People who die of illnesses that are in fact curable these days have only themselves to blame. The patient is admittedly a suicide risk—his official papers say so in black and white—but a cynical voice remarks: Who isn't at risk of suicide? Everyone knows that Othello's pathological jealousy and inferiority complexes were therapy-resistant. When Plácido Domingo played the dusky-skinned king of Venice, my singer sang beside him in the role of Desdemona. I know there've been several other singers who've sung Desdemona beside him, too. Polygamy is a basic principle of the theater. Was I jealous of Domingo? Not at all. I sat in the front row enjoying my soprano's voice. By the end, Othello was dead and I felt more alive than ever. A DVD proved far more effective a balm to my weary spirit than any medication. Only one question remained: Do we have to paint Othello black to understand his sufferings? The life force of the singer's skin shone through his makeup, which suited his striking features—and to this extent, the makeup artist did her work well—but still something bothered me. I didn't want to identify a character by his skin color, and above all, I didn't want to be forced to do so. Obviously, Othello's anger and vulnerability are related to discrimination. But it's not as if these feelings would disappear in a better society. Pathological jealousy will continue to exist, and I, too, could be an Othello. If we decided to paint every character a different color, the audience's powers of discernment would atrophy. For example, I wouldn't know what color to paint myself to be able to speak about Celan's sufferings. I'd wash my face in fresh water before giving my talk, but I would never put on white makeup. No one is white except a paper doll. Every human being should be allowed to keep their own skin color, which is always a mixture, ambiguous, and as ever-changing as happiness itself.

The name Othello begins with an *o* and ends with an *o*. Both letters are identical, round, and empty. On a chessboard, black-and-white thought patterns dominate. When one side wins, the other loses. There are black pieces and white pieces, no gray or red ones. Someone who's white can't be black. Is this logic really correct? Othello really ought to go into therapy, otherwise the hyperfunction of his organs responsible for the production of jealousy might cost several lives. He can't change society's black-and-white mode of thinking, but he might at least learn to take some deep breaths and release his anger. What can his wife Desdemona do? She doesn't go searching for a remedy to cure him. She sacrifices her life but doesn't become a saint after death.

It occurs to me that I've never once heard the word *heil* from my singer's lips. Neither in the form of healing (Heilung), nor a remedy (Heilmittel), nor sainthood (Heiligtum). As far as I know, she's pretty much never sung Wagner. Maybe she was Eva once in *Meistersinger*, but that's it. The next time I see her on the street, I'd like to ask the reason for this. Why no Wagner? Perhaps she didn't want to strain her voice by stretching it in so many different directions. Even early in her career she thought a lot about the decline of Maria Callas's voice that was attributed to singing Verdi and Wagner in quick succession. I don't know if this conjecture is true; I don't even have an opinion about what it means for a voice to decline. Celan trained his voice relentlessly, translating songbirds from different regions. With good cheer and confidence, he imitated the songs first of Mandelstam, then of Dickinson. Apollinaire was also in his repertoire, of course, along with Michaux. Neither Khlebnikov nor Mayakovsky was too much for his voice—on the contrary! Celan sang full-throatedly with his own voice when he translated. The only voice that seemed strange to him was, increasingly, his own; perhaps he'd taken a *breath-turn* and left his voice behind so he could plunge deeper and farther, unencumbered by baggage, into a space of art too narrow to admit an I. The narrowness of this strait was an advantage: even the most minimal vibration of the air could take the place of an aria.

A wooden puppet is hollow in the spot where the voice is produced. Woyzeck's body was hollow, too, because he had sold his body to modern medicine. At least he received a paycheck for this, unlike the laboratory bats. The viscera and the brain are the final assets remaining to those who've been written off as sick all their lives.

I enter the grand hall of the Metropolitan Opera. Even though it's a DVD, it smells different here than the Festspielhaus in Baden-Baden where I often go to see *Der Rosenkavalier*. The walls have a different odor, as do the opera-goers' garments. The companies that produce these digital discs haven't yet revealed their secret method for digitalizing odors. I'm so grateful to this recording that gives a pauper like me—incapable of affording a train ticket to Baden-Baden much less a flight to New York—access to these stages. It's odd: I used to be able to afford to go to the festival in Salzburg. Then a duration of time followed in which I spent virtually nothing and almost always stayed home. Any normal person would assume I was able to save money during this period, but my bank account dwindled. Well, you can always work if you need money! But that's precisely what I can't do. My hands remained empty.

A new friendship is my new form of long-distance travel. The airline is called Leo-Eric Fu and can fly much faster than any Lufthansa stork or the Indonesian divinity Garuda. Leo-Eric Fu, the grandson of a physician who practiced Chinese medicine in Paris and read Celan. His role: friend. His voice: tenor. His personal pronoun: you. Patrik falters; he can't remember if he's been using the informal *du* to address Leo-Eric instead of the formal *Sie*. No matter. Tomorrow, or the day after, his friend will become a *du*-you. Then the patient will stop feeling like a patient. His name: Patrik. His voice: baritone. He feels reborn. What has this marvelous Trans-Tibetan man done with Patrik? Nothing more than ask him questions, give him gifts, lend his thoughts wings. He'd like best to turn around on the spot and go back to the café to continue the dialogue. There's still so much to discuss regarding Celan. Patrik can no longer remember why he interrupted their conversation. Because of an appointment? Do I even have an appointment? It's true that now and then I'm obliged to claim I have an appointment. The appointment is my garden fence. Without it, anyone can wander into my garden at will and trample the green shoots of fragile new thoughts. An appointment is the only fence everyone instantly accepts. Even my girlfriend stopped undressing right away when I told her I had an appointment to get to. When was that? A Tuesday in the distant past. An appointment always has two shorelines. The other shore isn't permitted to be another woman, and I didn't have a male friend. Not yet anyhow. I was familiar with the term "customer consultation." All I had to do was become a customer, which I figured couldn't be so hard. Buying something automatically makes one a customer. Apart from emperors and beggars, anyone who wants to can easily become a customer. What should I buy today? A liter of milk. The coffee tastes burned without milk, I can't repeat often enough. But they don't give you an appointment to buy milk. I can't buy a car because the streets and intersections confuse me. I don't want to buy a vacation trip, the soles of my shoes are too thin. I lack the self-assurance to purchase insurance. My only chance would be to get a doctor's appointment. I called my primary care physician and asked to schedule a routine checkup. I don't feel like discussing my infirmities. Fortunately every human being is potentially sick, so you can ask for a checkup without specifying your symptoms.

I have a doctor's appointment! The effect this sentence had on my girlfriend was like a command from the highest echelons. In a single motion she tugged the jeans that had been coiling around her ankles back up to her waist. The indigo color swallowed first her calves, then her pink kneecaps with skin so thin you could imagine seeing the white bone, and finally her raven-black underpants. Women fall to pieces when they undress. When they get dressed again, a single unity is restored. I succeeded in stopping my girlfriend from overflowing and got her packed up again in clothes. She immediately believed I had a doctor's appointment. She didn't ask for details, sought no confirmation; she just picked up her handbag and left.

A past is inherently a third person, particularly when you're trying to play a first-person role in the present tense. Even the present is a constant deferment, a shaky photograph with blurred contours. The different times collide in your head, causing a throbbing pain. Doctors call the temples *tempora*. Colliding times, colliding temples. It hasn't been so long since the patient successfully expelled his girlfriend from his apartment with a doctor's appointment. Was it a week ago? A month? Maybe even a year? He's losing his sense of time, which doesn't bother him, as time can't be measured with the senses anyhow. Our sense of time is always imaginary. Timelessness, on the other hand, is definitely a real sensation. It began when all the concert halls closed. Before that, the patient could pick up complimentary flyers in the foyer containing the season's program and set them up on his desk like miniature folding screens. Now and then he even treated himself to a cheap ticket. Eventually the program contained only broken promises. Verdi was announced but he never showed up because the Italian border was closed. Neither Richard Strauss nor Tchaikovsky could travel to Berlin. Just names devoid of corporality. On the radio, they're saying all the opera houses and concert halls are open again, but the timelessness persists.

The patient won't need any more doctor's appointments. Now he has a friend he can make a date with. It isn't yet clear whether or not Leo-Eric will be his friend. The word *friendship* has a substantial heft to it. When something goes wrong, other heavyweight words come into play: words like *failure* and *betrayal*. In Russia, it's customary for a Lensky to visit his friend Onegin every day and spend more time with him than with his ladylove. It doesn't bode well to play with fire or friendship. A friendship can even cost a life. The patient shuts his eyes and hears the voice of Leo-Eric earnestly singing the tenor part. The patient would so love to play Eugene Onegin, who enjoys boredom as a luxury and conjures up sex appeal from the coldness of his heart. The baritone harbors something evil in his soul, like Don Giovanni, who's no longer seen onstage now that he has lost his #MeToo trial and is rotting away in a Spanish prison. Why are men who harass, abuse, and murder women permitted to sing onstage and enjoy public admiration? Why should men like this be allowed to sing beside my singer? Not quite as bad as Don Giovanni, but still a pathetic psychopath, this Onegin is unable to access his own emotions, so he childishly fires off his pistol in all directions. The patient wants to sing the baritone part so he'll be close to his soprano. He'll be an Onegin with no knife, money, or sex appeal. And he'll find a way around having to kill Lensky.

The prelude rises from the depths of the pit to stun the listener. A Tchaikovsky overdose. Tchaikovsky himself is innocent. It's a good thing he died back when Hitler was still pissing his pants and Stalin was waiting for his moustache to grow. After the war in Germany, no one let themselves find sweetness in the taste of bitter almond. A person telling a fairy tale couldn't be taken seriously, regardless if it was about swans or a nutcracker. It was seen as politically questionable to be lulled through repetition into a state of rapture. Even poetry was expected to wean itself off the sound of magical incantations. Celan cleansed his voice of the Eastern European sound that no longer pleased a West German ear. But was this really an Eastern European tone color and not a basic component of human civilization? Is there really some purely Jewish coloration that remains after you wash away the Slavic tint? And who was it trying to give Celan a proper scrub-down along with their own conscience?

The patient hurries home, where his Tatyana awaits him. When Tatyana falls in love with Onegin, he isn't prepared to give up his life of freedom for the sake of some village girl. His rejection pierces Tatyana's young heart like a knife; it's her first time experiencing such a wound. Instead of waiting for him to mature, she marries an older man of rank and fortune. When by chance Onegin runs into Tatyana years later, she's a polished diamond in high society. He falls in love with her and is rebuffed. The patient would have recognized Tatyana's potential in the first act, he wouldn't have waited until Act Three to confess his love. He can't understand why men—not just Onegin, also Alfredo and Othello—have to be so incredibly stupid to get cast as the lead, and why all their women are intelligent and unhappy.

Tatyana writes Onegin a long letter. This scene lasts all night. The singer sings in Russian, a language she cannot speak. She has learned this long text by heart, developing a deep attachment to the language without really learning it. The patient finds his breath constricted during the monologue. This song in a foreign tongue that is foreign not just to him but to the singer as well seizes him by the roots of all his nerve plants.

How many times now has the patient spent the night with Tatyana? He can scarcely breathe on account of the emotions constricting his chest, and by the end of the letter, tears pour from his eyes. He applauds loudly along with the audience living inside the digital disc. He imagines himself at the performance in Moscow, sitting high up on a side balcony. The president, who understands art as a national treasure, applauds loudly. The patient claps more loudly still. Other men on the balcony whose role it is to ensure the safety of the powers that be clap halfheartedly. The patient doesn't want his conspicuously loud applause to be interpreted politically. He just wants to pay his respects to the American soprano. Thanks to her, fewer people will now be able to claim that only Russians can truly understand Pushkin and sing Tchaikovsky. Plus no one in the audience witnessing this performance today will ever again think that Americans speak only a single language. The patient knows for a fact that the singer, who was born in Pennsylvania, is familiar with at least four languages. In Prague, the city of her ancestors, having several tongues wasn't anything out of the ordinary. But in the city of her birth, not so many people can go shopping in Italian, give charming answers to challenging interview questions in German, and feel at home in French.

Patrik's parents, who come from Ukraine, rarely cast a retrospective glance eastward. Patrik doesn't know any Ukrainian music, or even a single Ukrainian word. When Patrik used to ask his parents about Ukraine, they would respond evasively: What does this country have to do with you, you're from Frankfurt. His parents found it alienating that migration was such a frequent topic at Patrik's school. The parents' opinions rubbed off on their son. He kept his distance from these discussions and felt annoyed when someone asked if he was from Frankfurt an der Oder. He didn't want to be seen as a person from the East. To be an Easterner can mean so many things. Even East Berlin has a fairly Eastern location. Patrik, on the other hand, grew up in the metallic heart of Germany, home to the country's most significant airport, where skyscrapers steal space from clouds. He's proud of Frankfurt am Main because his American singer studied there, and so speaks an effervescent, supple German to this day.

The more often he reiterates that he's German, the more uncertain he becomes. No one asks him where his parents are from. But the police have started to record parental countries of origin on a blacklist. A person being German no longer suffices, in their view, to demonstrate the cleanliness of his underwear. Skin color is no guarantee either. The security system logs parental origins as an important piece of data. The patient won't be able to conceal his background any longer. Suddenly it occurs to him that Czernowitz, the birthplace of Paul Celan, is now a Ukrainian city. He's Celan's countryman! Finally some good news. He applauds with joy, even though there isn't any stage. He can't wait to tell Leo-Eric.

Patrik takes Leo-Eric's card out of his jacket pocket. His eyes flit across the street name and pause on the house number: 19. Fortunately a primary number. The five-digit zip code is secondary if not tertiary. No fault of the residents, of course. Under the name Leo-Eric Fu is the name of his institute with a telephone number. At the very bottom is a Chinese ideogram that Patrik can't read. One should always begin with the illegible. Patrik wrote this once in his notebook, the one with *Threadsuns* on the cover. He can't remember what became of that notebook. All he has now are a few loose index cards lying around his desk like so many business cards. You can't bind them together to make a book.

Should he build a house of cards and wait for a gust of wind? Score points at a conference with his loaded cards? What *charred* ideas.

Patrik does want to go to Paris, though—not for the conference, but to see the Paris meridian and grasp with his own two feet that there are various meridians. Through the thin soles of his shoes, he'll feel the *méridien de Paris* inlaid in the floor with colored stones. Where can he spend the night in Paris? Hotels are either overbooked, overpriced, or permanently closed. He'll sleep in a riverbed or a bed whose canopy is the sky. The thought that the sun's position in the sky depends on where and when it's being looked at robs him of gravity. A sun can be observed here and there at exactly the same time, since there are twelve suns, each of them describing their own cosmic career path. What was the Trans-Tibetan man trying to say? That the meridians can link separate body parts back together? Eye, beard, tooth, brain, heart, hand. In what order should these Celan words be read? The parts of the body aren't numbered. Sometimes a tooth registers pain, sometimes hands are cold. When the telephone rings, the heart starts racing before beads of perspiration form on the brow. Sometimes the patient wakes up with his back drenched in sweat. When every bedsheet reminds you of the plague, you can't simply accept history as a list of checked-off illnesses.

It feels to the patient as if he's carrying around his entrails awkwardly jumbled together in their string bag of nerves like vegetables on the way home from market. As a result, a green bean pierces the skin of an overripe tomato, while the eggs escape from their carton and rhythmically crack between two tins. We feel ashamed when something hurts. Still, it's easier to call in sick than to find a tree that will help the patient sort out the world. The tree's respectable branches grow in four directions, and no twig causes any pain to another. It would be better to have a tree in one's body instead of an aorta. Since the body parts are in disarray, they torment the nerves. Eye, beard, brow, tooth, brain, heart: were they born to call in sick? Most certainly not. I ought to leave my body to its own devices, it can lead a healthier life without me. Farewell, dear body! I'll stop trying to read my partial, physical pain. Instead, I'll read Celan. That would be the most sensible thing for me to do between the rising and setting of a sun. There are twelve suns, and each of them must be taken seriously. I don't want to be a customer or patient—I want to be a reader! Isn't that something I've wanted all along? Yes, of course, I wanted that from the very beginning, but I never got around to it because so many other things got in the way. I was always having to take care of this or that for other people. Instead of reading, I took an overcrowded local train to visit my lonely grandmother in the hospital. When I arrived, they told me she'd never been admitted. My journey was in vain. Then I was supposed to pick up my girlfriend's kid from preschool. When I got there, it was too late. The child had already been picked up. In front of the preschool, I was approached by a stranger who wanted to speak with me about the death of Christ. I was confused. Why did Jesus allow his living body to be put on display and reproduced in paintings if invisible values are what matters? I wished for nothing more than to become invisible so as to be able to read. To read Celan. Constantly I was prevented from doing so. I received an invitation from a literary club to give a talk about Nelly Sachs. I visited in order to clarify that I hadn't done any research on her. But at the club they said they hadn't planned anything on this poet and wouldn't be doing so in the future. It was a provocation, directed not against me but against literature in general. Why didn't they want to host a Nelly Sachs event? I voiced my disagreement to the people at the literary club, almost shouting. Nelly Sachs, I informed them, deserved wider recognition. She stuck it out in the postwar period for nearly the same length of time as Celan. Nelly Sachs died twenty-two days after him. It was the day on which Celan's dead body, which had been found in the Seine, was buried. She was twenty-nine years older than him and wanted to be his guardian angel, but she couldn't save his life. Who can succeed in being an angel, after all? The people at the literary club called the police and told the two officers who showed up soon after that I'd broken the club's plate glass display window with my fist. My hand was bleeding and splinters of glass glinted on the sidewalk. I didn't want to be seen as a crazy person. So I explained that I was trying to steal some of the books displayed in the vitrine. Better a thief than a madman. Only then did I notice the name Gottfried Benn in the display case. The arranged volumes were all books of poems, and all by Benn. I quickly said that I had made a mistake, and actually I didn't want to steal any books by this poet. The officers left without arresting me. I waste too much time on activities that don't lead anywhere. Now all I want to do is read. Celan's poem says: "But now!" The two words *but* and *now* don't fit together so well. They're about to part ways. Which one of them should I hold on to? But or now?

4. *The Cerebellum Worm and the Tree of Life*

Finally Patrik is once more sitting across from the person with whom he can speak about Celan. The conversation needs to begin, but how? *How are you?* That might be an appropriate opening. But against his will, a series of words pop up that sound more like a magic spell than a greeting.

"Eye, beard, tooth, brain, heart, throat, hand: How can I bring them together?"

Why doesn't Patrik ask how Leo-Eric is? It's good manners to play a proper prelude before drawing back the curtain to reveal the stage. But Leo-Eric shows no surprise at this idiosyncratic overture and responds calmly to the loud blast of baritone, nonchalantly entering Act One of this unknown drama. He sings the tenor part.

"The heart meridian. The heart, the throat, the eyes, and the hands all lie on the pathway of the heart meridian. Last time I shared a few things about the liver meridian. There are in total twelve principal meridians, and the heart meridian is one of them. Its most important branch runs from the heart through the esophagus up through the tissue of the eyeball."

The earnestness in the tenor's voice, his slight French accent along with his Trans-Tibetan features blend into a magical potion that makes Patrik tipsy. He asks in a faltering voice:

"This branch that ascends from the heart through the throat and eyes, does it go all the way to the brain?" Reclining against the pliant back of his white plastic chair with eyes half closed, Patrik articulates each word more precisely than necessary, as if to deprive these impatient words of their haste.

"I don't think this branch reaches the brain. By the way, my grandfather never used the word *brain*. He only ever referred to this organ as *the lake of marrow*."

"Lake of marrow?"

"The brain is filled with marrow."

"Where does this marrow come from?"

"I don't know exactly, but the large bones of the spine contain bone marrow."

"So the brain is nourished by the spine?"

"My grandfather occasionally remarked that the marrow lake's primary source of nourishment was heart blood. The heart meridian connects the heart with the eyeball tissue."

Hearing these words, Patrik feels an uneasy thirst.

His retinas are parched, even his assiduous blinking can't moisten them.

"Hearing the word *tissue* makes me immediately aware that my eyes are thirsty. I've got to drink something right away. Where's the server?"

"Are your eyeballs pounding like a heart?"

"There are three synchronized pomegranates pounding in my body: one heart and two eyes."

Leo-Eric appears not in the least dismayed by this formulation. Feeling encouraged, Patrik goes on speaking:

"My eyeballs are ticking like bombs. But please don't worry! I'm doing fine."

"Are your hands pounding as well?"

"No, that stopped. My hands are dead now that they've been operated on. I lay on the operating table, a bat with wounded wings, thinking: How strange—I'm not a Johann Strauss fan and it wasn't his operetta *Die Fledermaus* I was trying to see, it was *Arabella* by Richard Strauss. The opera houses keep changing their programs on short notice these days, so I had the good fortune to hear music that wasn't on my list. I was running late, it was already past the time when I was supposed to pick up the ticket I had ordered by phone. The bus driver said that according to the new immigration law, I wasn't allowed to ride the bus. That's odd, because I immigrated not after my birth but before: in other words, my parents were the immigrants. There was no time for a political discussion. I grabbed my rickety old bicycle and raced down the boulevard. Just as an ingenious idea occurred to me, a car sped over from the right, cutting me off. The brakes screeched and time stood still as my body was hurled into a dark future. I flew over the car, landing on the other side. Everything happened so fast I had no chance to decide how to fall. My hands were quicker than my brain; they wanted to protect my face and smashed against the sidewalk. After the operation, my hands worked perfectly again, at least as tools, but their connection to my heart was severed."

"What was the ingenious idea that caused the bicycle accident?"

Patrik feels ashamed to have used the word *ingenious*.

"The idea wasn't really so ingenious. I just thought: how wonderful that the letter *a* appears three times in the name Arabella! None of the characters have Teutonic names, and they're all rewarded by getting an A. Arabella, Mandryka, Adelaide, Zdenka, and Matteo. It's all very Viennese. In Vienna, Slavic and Italian influences are everywhere."

"Perhaps the letter *a* is somehow advantageous for opera singing, since it lets you open your mouth the widest?"

"I used to think so, too," Patrik replies. "But when

I observe the mouth of an opera singer, I see that she doesn't open it much wider for an *ah* than for other vowels. When she sings *ee,* on the other hand, her lips open incredibly wide horizontally. When I shout *ah* or *oh,* I open my mouth like a window and let the wind rush out from inside me. For the singer, it's very different, she has to keep the sound completely under control. A voice isn't wind."

"Every vowel touches on a different feeling when you examine it in isolation. I'm afraid of the German vowel *u*. It sounds ominous."

"At the same time there's something trustworthy about it. Think of the intimate *du*-you, for instance. It integrates the *u* sound very well."

"What about the *d*," Leo-Eric asks. "Is the dogmatic *d* in *du* advantageous for a friendship?"

"*D* comes from *denken* (think), which has many corners, spikes, and contours. *Denk dir!* Celan repeats this injunction to *think to yourself,* or *imagine,* four times in the last poem in *Threadsuns*. That's a huge difference from his "Death Fugue," where *we* and *he* take charge of the rhythm. *He* belongs to the group *we,* but there's also a *he* who's the master of destruction. All of this is fairly clear. But who is the *du* in the poem "Imagine"? It seems to me the second-person singular poses a danger to the first-person singular. A mirror-image illness. A pair of *d*'s: *Dorn* (thorn) and *Draht* (wire). A thorn causes pain, and a wire fence deprives people of freedom. A thorn gets stuck in an eye—but a wire can, despite everything, connect two people to one another. This poem is completely different from all the others in the book. The Six-Day War awakened the peat bog soldiers slumbering inside the poet. I thought they'd been dead and buried for decades, but I'm apparently mistaken. 'Israel must live, but this chain of wars that keep erupting...,' Celan writes to Franz Wurm, calling this thought 'one he can't think through to the end.' And it's no wonder he couldn't, seeing as the end still hasn't arrived fifty years after his death."

"A political poem?"

"Yes," Patrik says, "but with the letters of the alphabet as the main characters. The letter *d* in *denk* and *dir* is also the first letter of the verb *to die*."

"What about *to live*?"

"You can't live without inhabiting, and to inhabit you need a place. There are people who work hard with spade in hand to create a habitable spot on this earth. The letter *d* is contained in both *hand* and *world*. People march to a far-off land, they dig day and night and soon realize that they cannot succeed in making the spot habitable. Their eyes and forms were stolen a long time before. They can't even be buried. This all exists in the poem with the thinking *d*."

"Even my grandfather stayed glued to his radio when the Six-Day War began," says Leo-Eric. "It started when he heard about the Israeli air force striking Egyptian military bases without warning."

"Back then you learned about everything from the radio. I would prefer radio to the internet. I can think more calmly and rationally about an event when I'm not being bombarded with colorful video clips. As a young child, I was thrown off by the visual beauty of the bombs. When I see the word *Threadsuns,* something automatically clicks inside me."

"How am I to understand that?"

"The word reminds me of a particular sort of bomb that shoots white threads into the air. When I think of it, I actually see explosions above my head. My therapist once said it was a shame the word *paranoia* has gone out of style, because certain patients much prefer this word to the more fashionable ones floating around these days."

"My grandfather said it hardly took anything at all for Celan to hear the iron chain of wars clanking. To most people, that just looked like paranoia."

"I refuse to synchronize my heartbeat with a ticking war-bomb. I need a different system to govern my organs. Where did we leave off? Where do the other branches of the heart meridian lead? Is there a connection to the hands?"

"Yes, of course. The principal branch runs from the heart to the lung, curves across the upper arm then down to the pit of the elbow, terminating in the palm of the hand."

While Leo-Eric is explaining, his delicate fingers trace out a pathway from his chest to the crook of his elbow. He briefly dips into a memory that appears to slumber in a distant past, leaving Patrik alone in the present. Like a lonely, abandoned child, Patrik speaks softly to the back of his own left hand, which he addresses as *du*.

"You do everything for me, dear hand. My hand opens the apartment door, turns on the faucet, pushes the walls away when they try to crush me."

Leo-Eric wakes from his memory and asks, somewhat alarmed:

"What walls?"

"Well, it's not as if there's such a thing as a room with a fixed size."

"There isn't?"

"A room can go rogue and turn against me. The walls encroach on me, and the windows shrink."

"How can walls turn against you?"

Asking this question, Leo-Eric discreetly switches from the formal *Sie* to the intimate *du*-you. Patrik rejoices, secretly trembling, but at the same time two details interfere with his pleasure. First, the subject of the sentence wasn't him, it was the walls; and the *du*-you was the object of the antagonistic preposition *against*. Not the best start for a friendship. Patrik doesn't have the courage to voice his misgivings. Instead, he continues to elucidate his theory of space.

"If a space expands internally, this creates narrowness inside, a sort of strait, and there's no room left for me. If, however, the inverse occurs and space expands outward, it leaves me with nothing to hold on to."

Leo-Eric turns his palms that were lying on the table to face upward and responds with unexpected severity.

"The fact is, you want to write about Celan, but you fear this is beneath you, so this poetically threatening situation has been deflected to your private life. Your seemingly interesting observations are just a pale reflection of great art. You even leave out the artist's name."

Feeling himself attacked for the first time, Patrik holds his tongue. His friend has only just addressed him as *du*-you, and already he's analyzing his theory of space as a shortcoming.

"Please don't take offense," Leo-Eric says. "I've watched young, talented individuals crash and burn a number of times now. It was always too late when I was called in to help. This time I intend to be ruthless in conjugating your future tense."

"What do you mean? I don't quite understand."

"Here we are, sitting across from one another. You are Stockholm, I am Paris."

Patrik smiles weakly but not without pleasure, feeling the tiny screws of the wooden frame pressing against his skull loosen and turn. This is the wooden frame his mother once used for embroidery. She would sit leaning against the wall, immersed in her needlework. He didn't have the courage to address her shoulder blades. Perhaps he was afraid she wouldn't turn around, even if he called out to her at the top of his lungs.

"If I were Stockholm and you were Paris, the shortest line connecting us wouldn't pass through the Earth's center," Leo-Eric adds.

"True," says Patrik. "No epistle can pass through the hot magma that makes up the Earth's core. Letters always glide across its surface. Celan wrote many letters. Tons of them. I can't imagine one person being able to write so many letters," Patrik says.

"Letters were necessary for survival. Rage, pain, and fear needed to flow, not stagnate," the physician's grandson replies.

"I've been experiencing several forms of stagnation. Writing is impossible. I'm blocked. Maybe I should try acupuncture, but I'm afraid of pain, or more precisely, I'm afraid of the idea that I could possibly experience pain. Having one's fingers treated with needles is surely painful. My hands are oversensitive. Even just opening a letter makes them bleed."

Leo-Eric touches Patrik's fingertip with the tips of his own fingers and says, "It doesn't hurt. Your hand can manage everything without pain: opening letters, writing a text, or shaking a friend's hand. Do you feel pain?"

"No."

"This is where the heart meridian meets the meridian of the small intestine."

Patrik pulls his hand away, feeling ashamed that he can't endure harmless physical contact for very long. Wanting to leave the embarrassing moment behind as quickly as possible and transition to the next act, he says:

"In 1884, there was a major international meridian conference, and ever since, the meridian plane passing through the Royal Observatory in London has been considered the prime meridian. There were other meridians before this, but being recognized as a zero meridian isn't the point here. There are many meridians, and they would never cross if they all ran through the North and South Poles."

"Precisely," Leo-Eric says. "Celan wasn't interested in the axis the world as a whole spins around. He had a very personal understanding of the meridian despite his cosmic and cosmopolitan orientation. What climate zones will we reach if we extend the line connecting Paris and Stockholm?"

"Maybe the Amazon rainforest in Brazil? The tropics make me triste. Words shouldn't be read as metaphors. Whoever does that will—how did that literary critic put it?—get stuck in the underbrush of dead words. Words like *beard* and *tooth*."

"Why beard and tooth?"

"*Bart* and *Zahn* both appear in *Threadsuns* and have four letters."

Leo-Eric strokes his own smooth chin and says:

"Once as a small child I had an excruciating toothache and went running to my grandfather who told me to go to the dentist right away. My all-powerful grandfather, who could relieve me of any sort of discomfort, sent me to a doctor who worked with pliers and drills! I was horrified."

"Isn't there acupuncture for toothaches?"

"You can alleviate the pain, but you can't do anything to fix the tooth. The tooth is too hard."

"Celan thought of the soul as being as hard as a tooth. You need both of them to sing. Have you ever seen a singer without teeth? Never, it's impossible. A singer has to have good teeth. Josephine, for example, is a wonderful singer. Some people find her voice strange, like the voice of a bat. And as long as we're talking about Kafka: A jackdaw doesn't need a single tooth to sing."

Leo-Eric laughs, he seems to enjoy Patrik's constant leaping around and derailments. In this spirit, he asks:

"And the beard? Doesn't the jackdaw need a beard to sing?"

"No! Kafka was adamantly opposed to growing a beard, probably because his father had one. He kept a shaving mirror on his desk, as if being clean-shaven were necessary for writing."

"Is there something patriarchal about a beard for Kafka?"

"Not necessarily. Oskar Baum had a beard, and so did Felix Weltsch."

"Interesting. In *Threadsuns* there's the line: *the lightbeard of the patriarchs.*"

"That's not in *Threadsuns,* it's in *No Man's Rose.* In *Threadsuns* there's just the word *lightbearded,* or more precisely, *light-bearded,* separated by a hyphen, which appears in 'September, Frankfurt.' Freud's forehead makes a cameo in this poem. Maybe the beard also belongs to him?"

Patrik is astonished to discover that certain book pages, either from *No Man's Rose* or *Threadsuns,* are visible on the display screen in his head, as clear as a photograph. Could he possibly have an eidetic memory? In everyday life, he can't remember even the simplest things, such as whether or not he's ended his relationship with his girlfriend. On the other hand, there are certain poems he'll never forget—they've become part of his veins and sinews, and their words autonomously continue to forge new links and networks, like words in a foreign language recombining as you sleep. Patrik's favorite singer writes about this process in her autobiography. She believes that, above all, foreign languages continue growing in your brain during the night without any effort on the part of the sleeping individual.

"What are you thinking about right now?" Leo-Eric asks.

"Poems have been at work inside me ever since I stopped working on them. They're like foreign languages. Really, someone ought to research the connection between sleep and foreign languages. Poetry itself is a foreign language. It's my main source of nourishment, and sometimes I nourish it too."

"It's dangerous to work on poetry in your sleep. You aren't in control! You're better off practicing an active form of scholarship. Don't just let yourself get swallowed up!"

"We all get swallowed up sooner or later. There are people who fall silent when this happens, and others who sing."

"If you don't give your talk at the Celan conference, you'll be one of the silent ones."

"Scholars aren't supposed to sing."

"Who's forbidden you to sing?"

"No one's forbidding me to do anything; we live in a highly democratic country. First they invite me, then they drop me. I've lost my taste for this little game. I'd rather just stay in my apartment."

"You've just reminded me of Saint Jerome. He reads old manuscripts in a dark, gloomy chamber. A skull sits on his desk. A ray of sunlight enters the room, tinting his beard a fiery blond. In the past, I thought of an old scholar's beard as a clump of matted, gray thought-fibers. But this beard looks like the lush, thick hair of a vivacious woman. Is that what a light-beard is?"

"Sigmund Freud's beard looks pretty bourgeois in that photograph: gray and well-groomed."

"The brightness of his beard has a different source: the flashlight of psychoanalysis. You know something about that. What did you find in the dark cave of childhood?"

How does Leo-Eric know Patrik has seen a therapist? He knows everything, like an angel watching over the city from above seven days a week. There's no point hiding anything from him.

"To be honest, I've profited more from Freud literarily than medically."

"But you were in treatment once, weren't you?"

"My expectations were too high. I wanted to hear my mother sing the lullaby about the cockchafer that flies in May, but the therapist said he wasn't a shaman and couldn't raise the dead. He couldn't do what I wanted, and I didn't know what he wanted. During the therapy session, I mostly maintained a *hard silence,* pressing my lips together and wishing I had a great big beard to hide my intentions in. I started saying *beard silence* instead of *hard silence.* The beard is a sort of burqa concealing a proud masculine silence. By remaining silent, you obliterate your conversation partner. That's why Celan writes of a *blind silence.*"

"Singing would be better than silence if speaking is impossible. Or is that too cultural-political a thought? Please forgive me—this is a constant danger in my profession."

"As long as a person can sing, they should sing. In the case of the jackdaw—I mean in Kafka's case—the issue was the tuberculosis attacking his larynx. You might think an author doesn't need a physical voice since he can write, but that's wrong."

"If Kafka hadn't already been weakened by influenza, the tuberculosis wouldn't have killed him so quickly, according to my grandfather. The pandemic robbed Celan of two authors: Kafka and Apollinaire."

A human-sized shadow creeps from East to West, briefly casting its shade on the café guests before moving on and surrendering them to the sunlight. Patrik locates a fish-shaped cloud in the sky, loses sight of his friend's face, and thinks: What if Leo-Eric isn't really sitting here and this is all just taking place in my imagination? The twittering of the municipal birds suddenly ceases, and Patrik feels obliged to fill in for them.

"How awful it would be to lose the ability to sing but still have to remain a bird! I would let the letters sing in my place. The letters will go on singing even after our time has come to an end."

"How spooky! A world full of singing voices without a single living person?"

"Earth is already populated with the dead. Their songs aren't always beautiful, but they're certainly worth listening to."

"What would you sing as a person who isn't yet dead?"

"Maybe a song about a cockchafer in September, or some other insect ditty from beyond the grave. In Celan's early poems, he sang the nursery rhymes of the dead. A mixed chorus will burrow in my intestines. My fingertips will freeze, the tips of my toes, too—and at the same time, my head will boil in solitary polyphony. Using numbers to orient myself would work better. Count the letters, count the nuts! Not just almonds, count the peanuts and walnuts, too! You can't crack them, just count them. I've counted and recounted them all. Eye, beard, tooth, brain, heart, throat, hand: *Auge, Bart, Zahn, Hirn, Herz, Hals, Hand*. I offer you this medley of nuts without articles or possessive pronouns, just four letters each."

"Where did you find them? Only in *Threadsuns*, or did you go hunting in *Lightduress* too?"

"*Threadsuns*. My first plan was to use a sunbeam as a thread to stitch the poet's disintegrating body parts back together, like a surgeon."

"The sun's thread works for surgical sutures?"

"Sure! But I don't know how to cut or sew. All I can do is count."

"Why four letters and not three or five?

"Three is impoverished. In *Threadsuns*, the arm is the only body part with three letters. The hand has four."

"And five fingers."

The two men laugh unisono. A studenty-looking waitress suddenly stands beside Patrik, interrupting the conversation.

"What can I get you?"

A phrase like this would sound more natural on the lips of an older, sterner person.

"Blood-orange juice, please!" Patrik answers spontaneously, and only afterward does it occur to him to wonder why the word *Blut* (blood) wasn't included on his list of four-letter words. Probably because there's no such thing as pure blood. Blood always appears as part of a compound: *Blutstunden* (blood hours), *Bluthufe* (blood hooves), *Hellblut* (bright blood). With lightning-swift fingers, Patrik flips through the volume of poems in his memory. The waitress, to whom these efforts remain invisible, gives a matter-of-fact response:

"We don't have blood-orange juice."

"Then I'd like pomegranate juice, please! That's the only fruit that appears in *Threadsuns*."

"We don't have that either. I could offer you a grapefruit juice."

In the waitress's eyes, a faint irritation is germinating, while her speech maintains a dusty courteousness.

"Why grapefruit juice? The grapefruit available in Berlin is mostly imported from Israel. Celan didn't go to Israel until 1969."

The waitress ignores the guest's words and turns to face Leo-Eric, in the hope of finding him more user-friendly.

"Shall I just bring your friend a grapefruit juice? And for you? What would you like?"

"I would like a krater."

"I beg your pardon?"

"The krater was a sort of jug the Ancient Greeks used to mix wine with water. This, too, is a Celan word, it seems to me. The wine intoxicates, and the water has a sobering effect."

"Oh, I see, you'd like a wine spritzer. Large or small?"

The waitress softens her facial features. Perhaps she's pegged the two men as pot-smoking tourists, to be treated with indulgence. She turns her back on them and speaks with customers at the next table. Patrik's gaze snags on the angelic shoulder blades visible through the sheer rayon of her blouse.

"That woman's shoulder blades are so pretty, but unfortunately her tongue has grown hard."

Casually commenting on the waitress's physical appearance makes Patrik feel like a carefree teenager checking out random women with a friend. This moment of arrogant pleasure doesn't last long. Ashamed, Patrik lowers his eyes and says in a low, trembling voice:

"As you see, my mind is full of thought-foam."

"There's no need to be ashamed of foam. What would a life without foam look like? Foam protects my skin from the razor blade, it keeps my cappuccino warm and my beer fresh."

In Patrik's eyes, his new friend suddenly takes on the appearance of a man who shaves in the morning and drinks a nice cold glass of beer in the evening. At night he smooths his skin with the beaten egg whites offered to him by dream-women.

"And now what are you thinking?"

"My brain is like a storage closet full of junk—it's utterly unsuitable as an organ of thought. What organ should I think with when my brain is indisposed? The stomach has a more important function than thinking, as do the lungs. The heart is too exhausted."

"Why is your heart exhausted?"

"Because I've used it as a metaphor too many times."

"Do you know the poem 'VISIBLE, at brainstem and heartstem'?"

"Of course! *The midnight marksman pursues the twelvesong through the marrow of treason and putrefaction.* Do you suppose there are twelve songs the way there are twelve meridians?"

"I wanted to show you this book." Leo-Eric pulls out a paperback from his leather briefcase, his delicate fingers flipping through its pages, and stops at an anatomical illustration of the human head.

"Look here, Number 13 is the spinal cord. It's an extension of the medulla oblongata, Number 12. This bridge here is called the pons. Behind the pons you can see a little worm, the cerebellar vermis, beside the arbor vitae: the tree of life. Splendid, don't you think?"

Squinting, Patrik reads the words written in tiny ant letters.

"Splendid indeed! Pons, cerebellar vermis, arbor vitae. Are these medical terms? Is this a book on Chinese medicine?"

"It's a standard reference work of general medicine, and these terms aren't Chinese, they're Latin. Take medulla, for example, the Latin word for marrow. Look what it says here: 'The medulla oblongata is a region of the brainstem continuous with the pons above and the spinal cord below.'"

"Celan writes: *marrow of treason and putrefaction.*"

"If you want to reach inside another human being, the marrow is the deepest you can go."

"Do you know a lot about medicine?"

"No, I'm only repeating what my grandfather taught me. I'm not even in a position to accurately reproduce his words."

Leo-Eric flips forward a few pages until he finds a simplified drawing of the brain.

"Here are the words *brainstem* and *cerebral cortex.* This is the book Celan read as a psychiatric patient."

Leo-Eric closes the book and hands it to his friend. *Der Körper des Menschen: Einführung in Bau und Funktion* (*The Human Body: An Introduction to*

Structure and Function). The book was published by the respected scientific press Georg Thieme. Patrik gives the copyright page and foreword a quick glance. The first edition came out in 1966. The author Adolf Faller appears to be Swiss.

"Was this Celan's copy? Did you inherit it from your grandfather?"

Leo-Eric smiles with casual pride. "This isn't the original. My grandfather bought the same book and marked all the passages Celan had marked in his own copy. Here, for example: Celan underlined the words *aortic arch*. That's why my grandfather underlined this term here."

"Was he translating the traces of Celan's reading?"

"Exactly."

Patrik leafs through the book and finds the underlined words *bright blood*.

Lightly touching the book, Leo-Eric says: "On the inside of the cover, there's a poem by Celan. I always assumed my grandfather copied it from a printed book. But no! At the German Literature Archive in Marbach, which owns Celan's original copy of the reference book, I was able to confirm that my grandfather even copied Celan's handwriting. Celan himself wrote this poem."

Patrik stares at the handwriting—a copied Celan. *Near, in the aortic arch.* The poem, written in pencil, looks like hastily jotted notes. How to read a word isn't yet firmly established. Where you expect one letter, there might be two. The last line is curious: *214, that light.*

"I know this poem, but I don't remember seeing the number 214 in it."

"It really does look like 214. In fact, the word written there is *Ziv*."

The head of the *z* is much too round, and the final letter tips to the right.

"*Ziv*! Now I remember that word. What does it mean?"

"My grandfather said this is a Hebrew word."

"Oh, of course. There are always several languages present at the same time with Celan, both in his silences and song."

"Didn't he once say he didn't believe in bilingualism in poetry?"

"He was probably just in a bad mood. The critics who rejected the idiosyncrasies of Celan's writing abused the notion of bi- or multilingualism. Conservative readers wouldn't permit a 'real' German writer to make use of inscrutable metaphors or Eastern melodies, but since Celan had one foot in a foreign-language sphere, they were prepared to grant him a certain license. The hypocrisy and condescension of these 'supporters' infuriated the poet. He didn't want to be marginalized in these faux-liberal terms."

"Still, wasn't he overreacting?"

"Art is always an overreaction. Celan was writing in the middle of the world of multilingualism. In my opinion, he didn't just translate, he sang in his translations. He sang in Romanian, Russian, French, Hebrew, and English until he had no voice left. That was the point of departure for his late poetry. It begins with voicelessness."

"It's really a shame you aren't going to Paris."

"I can't formulate my talk in such a way that no one will be insulted."

"Is that the goal of scholarship—to avoid insulting anyone?"

"The word *goal* is already enough to make me flip out."

"If you like, I can lend you another book next time: *The Chinese Written Character as a Medium for Poetry* by Ernest Fenollosa and Ezra Pound. This was another volume on Celan's shelf. From the point of view of multilingualism, it's certainly an interesting work. Can you read Chinese?"

"No."

"No matter. Some poets read Chinese characters without knowing them. Victor Segalen, for example."

Patrik smiles and thinks about how he's going to touch foreignness with his bare hands—isn't that the royal road to poetry?

5. *Colliding Times*

Patrik is walking. Walking is a process in which beginnings are always shrouded in fog. How did he say goodbye to his friend at the café? Did he finish his blood-red juice? He can't remember anything except that Leo-Eric lent him the medical reference book. This treasury of anatomical words is astonishingly heavy for a paperback volume.

Patrik must get home, where no one's waiting for him but Richard Strauss. The more the walker thinks, the longer his path grows. Behind the rhythm of his walking, Octavian's voice asserts itself. *Who, you, were, who, you, are, no, one, knows, no, one, gues, ses*: each syllable a step. In Patrik's imagination, he's already home, his trembling, addicted hands tearing open the DVD case, and already he's allowed to gaze into the narrow goldmine of the orchestra pit. Sometimes music is as blind as the human heart. It doesn't always notice when a prisoner is being forced to dig his own grave right next door. What was the composer unable to see, and what was he unwilling to see? The string instruments are all the honey-sweet colors of wood, the musicians white-breasted with black backs like orcas. One can still hear isolated attempts to find the concert pitch A. Then the conductor appears and receives respectful applause, an advance payment for services to be rendered. In reality, Patrik isn't yet sitting in the audience, his shoes still have a great many cobblestones to traverse.

It really shouldn't be so difficult to go home. You just roll up the path you've taken like a long, narrow rug that automatically returns you to your point of departure. There's no art to finding one's way home. So why is homecoming the subject of so many artworks? Come home, Mother cries. She wants her son to quickly roll up the stained carpet of his life and return to his ancestral home. The choice he faces is either to hurl himself into the arms of the nearest woman or retreat to his dead mother's womb.

A person who can continue to distance himself from home, one step farther each day, is no longer a patient. Patrik isn't a patient, since now he has a friend—a friend, moreover, who has entrusted him with a family treasure. Leo-Eric's grandfather copied the traces left behind by his favorite poet into this book with his own hand, and now Patrik is allowed to take the book home with him. It's as if he's carrying around a piece of 1960s Paris.

Patrik hurries to return to his own four walls. He loves his apartment; more precisely, he loves his house number: seventeen, a prime number that can be divided only by the number one (the highest authority) and by itself, seventeen.

He counts the steps, counting and climbing; his counting drives the climbing. When he has counted forty-seven steps, his key slides into the lock. His apartment is located directly beneath the hirsute roof. A small, dim skylight is the only aperture to the out-of-doors; when the sky cooperates, the apartment becomes more than a dreary hole. Straw-yellow weeds sprout between the roof tiles. A sparrow slices the blue rectangle in two. Patrik takes off his jacket. He thought the jacket would make him Upstanding Citizen Patrik. Apparently, the opposite is true. The jacket forces him to look like someone, and that distracts him from himself. Wearing his jacket, he's The Patient, because he doesn't outwardly appear to have any other profession. Without the jacket, he can just be Patrik, a name filled with nothing.

He hangs the jacket on a hook attached to the wall with two nails. The nail heads look like the round eyes of an owl. Its intelligent silver eyes attentively watch to see what Patrik will do next. The telephone rings, Patrik flinches as if an electric wire has touched his skin. It's impossible, the phone can't be ringing. The cord is unplugged and lies curled on the floor like a murdered snake with a broken neck. The ringtone slices into the veins of time, no matter if it's reenacting a Mozart melody or the shrieks of seagull chicks. Time bleeds—its aorta has been nicked. Patrik goes back to being a patient, he crawls across the floor, pulls out the cord, and tosses the plug aside. Someone's been sneaking into my apartment in my absence and plugging in the phone. I never give anyone my phone number because no one ever asks for it. Besides the sparrow singing modestly on cue and the sound of the electric kettle, silence should reign in my apartment until a DVD transforms it into an opera house. The ringing telephone is a stain upon our cultural history, a blot in a musical score, a violent attack on the ear. The wall outlet gazes at me in childish supplication with its innocent black eyes. I look at the prongs of the plug; in a flash it occurs to me that maybe it was the singer who was trying to call. Not long ago I wrote her a letter and sent it to her care of Symphony Hall in Boston, where she was scheduled to perform. No doubt this concert was canceled like the others. Besides, the singer has been in Berlin this whole time. I often see her on the street, and I could have just handed her the letter in person. The letter wasn't returned to me from America, so possibly it was forwarded. My letter was at least as passionate as Tatyana's letter to Onegin. To be honest, I stole some of Pushkin's sentences. But since these were my own mistranslations from the Russian, copyright infringement isn't a concern. At the end of the letter I added my phone number. I plug the cord back into the jack. After all, plug and jack belong together like yin and yang. If someone calls me now, it can only be the singer. Delusions of grandeur, I know. But one thing is certain: the probability of *her* calling me is far greater than that of any other diva calling me. As a young woman, the singer saw how cold-heartedly famous artists dismissed their fans. She resolved never to behave in such a way if she herself became famous. Whether or not she actually reserves sufficient time for each fan is another question. Still, it's already extraordinary of her to have given thought to the matter. After all, she's a diva, not a priest.

The night I spent composing the letter gleams in my memory like no other. For the span of one night, I was Tatyana writing a long love letter to Onegin. The intoxicating hours made me feel utterly fulfilled, unlike any other night I had hitherto experienced, for which reason it would have been better to throw the finished letter into the fire instead of bothering the singer with it. She doesn't need to meet me. Without noticing that I exist, she reveals to me a vast human landscape every night. Without her, my room would contract even further, eventually obliterating me. Thanks to her, I can—despite my illness—walk long distances and laugh out loud. Every human being needs a great, unrequited passion to enrich their life with impossibility. Old-fashioned? Being old-fashioned isn't enough for me. I'd like to be the contemporary of Petrarch and Shakespeare. Or, even farther back, Hippocrates, the oldest person to appear in *Threadsuns*. He was obsessed with the number four, just like me. Using a marker, I wrote the four qualities *warm, cold, dry, moist* on the four corners of my desk. Accordingly, I always place my cup of hot coffee at the front left, cold mineral water at the back left, books at the back right, and at the front right the handkerchief for wiping my tears. I'm incapable of crying. How long has it been since I last wept? Warm and moist: the red heart; warm and dry: the yellow liver; cold and dry: the black spleen; cold and moist: the white brain. The patient sings Hippocrates's chart like a nursery rhyme. It reassures him when things can be assigned to one of four directions. Finally he can stop walking and can be enclosed by four walls. One wall is sweet, the second bitter, the third sweet-and-sour, the fourth salty. Hippocrates thought, much like the Chinese in antiquity, that the parts of our body correspond to the cosmos, which we perceive as color, taste, and temperature. A person with the right expertise can serve as a conductor for the organs and keep the body fluids flowing.

Somnolent or insomniac, the patient goes to bed while it's still light out. His four limbs orient themselves with respect to the four corners of the bed, and he begins to speak with his fifth limb. Where is this fifth limb supposed to go? Should it go looking for a woman with whom not just this one member but the entire organism can live as a parasite? The bed is rectangular just like a book. Does this make the bedsheet a suitable backdrop for reading erotic medical poems? The patient doesn't even have to open the book, many of whose poems he has internally scanned. Two of them are unchaste, a word he never would have thought to use if Celan hadn't used it first.

Pursuing unchaste trains of thought is a desperate attempt to pump the last serviceable hormones from the body. To reach this goal, one interprets being stabbed in the heart as a sign of infatuation and a fatty tumor on the nape of the neck as a female hand approaching for a caress. The war's been over for decades, but the front door still tastes burned. Or is it just my sooty tongue? The transformation of wood into charcoal can't be rewound like a tape. Outside, a fire alarm goes off. The patient jumps out of bed. The war isn't over yet. He presses the book Leo-Eric lent him to his chest. The underlined words mustn't get lost in the chaos of war. Through the small, dirty windowpane, the patient glimpses a house-slipper cloud. Far and wide, not a bomb in sight. Relieved, the patient opens the medical tome. On page six, sexuality is explained with two letters, X and Y, followed by several drawings of an embryo. According to medical science, these two chromosomes transform directly into the embryo. There's no explanation of what happens in between. Did Celan skip over the portrayal of the embryo, or feel transported back to the time of the not-yet-born?

Many poets have praised the splendor of their beloveds, but Celan alone mentions the female erectile tissues. What happens when the heart starts racing, when blood flows more forcefully through belly and thighs, and the silken curtain begins to swell? Medical professionals speak of *commissure,* and Celan uses this word, too, so basically it's a matter of the intercourse between a you and an I. Street traffic is also a form of intercourse, which did nothing to spoil Celan's pleasure, as it could serve as a detour when rejection loomed. He speaks of a *no access zone.* But it's not so much a refusal of access as a toll. Anyone who pays the toll is permitted to proceed. This is a firefly, he says. Why call it a fly? The Italian word for firefly, *lucciola,* has an additional meaning: prostitute. The poet's mother—the one who sang him the song about the cockchafer—was murdered. Ravaged body landscape with shards. People used to smash clay figures and bury the shards in the four corners of a field: a ritual for a good harvest. They smashed the female doll's limbs and now she's digging her own grave. This isn't a ritual for a good harvest: it's a crime. The doll is me. My classmates shattered the doll. I wasn't even able to determine whether I was victimized deliberately. After this incident, I would lock myself in the bathroom during recess and take a different detour home each day. Either my safety precautions worked perfectly or it was never their intention to make me a routine victim. I am still alive, and my mother is not.

The patient registers mild pain: the sharp edge of the book presses against his left wrist. When the term *cerebral cortex* pops up in his brain, he rifles through the book in a panic, finding the term right away, as if he already knew its location. Celan underlined it; Leo-Eric's grandfather underlined it; and now it's the patient's turn to read it, interpret it, and share it with others.

The brain wears a mantle to shield itself from humankind's coldness. I don't run around with my brain exposed, so I'm less at risk than a person who attends every single conference and projects the interior of their brain on a screen. After the presentation, I sidestep the group dinner with other participants, but that doesn't mean I go drinking on my own near the conference venue or visit a bordello to wash the bad taste from my mouth. Let the fireflies remain on the riverbank—I don't head in their direction. I don't leave my apartment, and I refuse to sacrifice my liver for seventh heaven. I am disturbed by Celan's body odor, which suddenly emanates from the anatomy textbook. The poet produces his masculine milk in the gall bladder, and his gaze trembles along the contours of a woman's hip, though the woman doesn't exist. Why is he alone? He's been transformed into a monstrous creature whose presence no one can bear. Isolation is a death sentence in disguise. Is it a form of punishment to be turned into a monster? Hippocrates said that illness wasn't a punishment imposed by God. Medicine's first step was to acquit the ill.

I'm not a sacrificial animal, and the anatomy book isn't a slaughterhouse. The 1960s drawings, tinted a pale pink, repose gently and modestly upon the page. Heart, liver, brain: I find the images reassuring. Perhaps Celan, too, flipped through this anatomical book like a child with a picture book at bedtime. Sorcerers, witches, and monsters will protect the sleeper from the nightmare of genocide. Anatomy offers a reassuring sense of order: each organ has its place. Besides, a liver is just a liver, nothing more, nothing less. The liver's job is to remove toxins, a task it performs in the dark with great precision in the absence of lamp and clock. You can't see your own liver, nor the liver of the person you're talking to. If I were ever to behold many livers at once and count my own as the seventeenth, it would mean my soul is journeying through the air. I am flying over a battlefield full of bloody, ripped-open bellies. I fly among vultures and angels, caught up in a whirlwind I can't escape, trying with my last ounce of strength to count the bodies.

Celan's poem "DETOUR- / MAPS" and the *seventeenth liver* transport the patient back to a boyhood where studying various kinds of bombs kept a vague fear at bay. World War II ended long before the patient's birth. But he still feels as if he grew up surrounded by weapons of war, he even knows the bombs' nicknames—Hailstone, Little Radish—and is familiar with the ten-hundredweight bomb that appears in Celan's poem. As a child, Patrik spent his winter evenings reading war novels he found on a trash heap. He immersed himself in the flaming metropolis, and when he shut the book and went to bed, he would suddenly feel *phosphorus fear*. During sleepless nights, he would secretly slip out of the house, sit on a swing in the little neighborhood park, and stare at the dark sky until cosmic capillaries appeared. The phosphorus bomb used during the Second World War by both the Germans and

English was nicknamed Christmas Tree because of the countless white threads falling to the ground in a pyramid shape. The phosphorus stuck to human skin and slowly, excruciatingly burned through to the marrow. In this respect, the Christmas Tree clearly resembles the mushroom cloud of an exploding atomic bomb. In *Lightduress*, Celan writes to *a brother in Asia*. That lethal radiance in the sky will go on producing meridians of pain long after the poet's death.

One day the patient heard on the radio that phosphorus grenades were being used in Iraq. The American military received international condemnation and issued a statement explaining that these weapons hadn't been conventionally deployed but rather were being used as incendiary devices intended not to kill but merely to illuminate the city, allowing for surgical strikes. As phosphorus ignites on contact with oxygen, a phosphorus bomb doesn't need a detonator.

At some point, the patient stopped reading war novels and studying weapons. He stowed these books that had outlived their usefulness on the top shelf of his least accessible bookcase and left them to gather dust. When he moved to Berlin, he didn't take any of these volumes with him; there was only room for a few books in his duffel bag, and he remembers packing Schnitzler, Musil, and Bernhard.

His younger brother found the war novels and books about weaponry on the bookshelf. After his parents banned violent computer games, he would spend his lonely evenings with these inherited volumes. He learned far more about bombs than his older brother; he even claims to have made some himself, so as to "set fire to the Sodom that is Berlin."

The shape of a bomb is inspired by the body shape of sharks, dolphins, and whales. It's no wonder that a trio of falling bombs looks like three whales. When the patient is walking outside and sees the shadow of a bomb on his own foot, he panics and quickly looks for an air-raid cellar. There's a subway station with inconspicuous metal doors. Behind these locked doors is a fountain of eternal health. The patient knows this means it's an air-raid cellar, but the bouncer turns him away. Not just anyone can take shelter here. Why won't you let me in? Because there's a limited number of seats, and regardless of what criteria are used, the patient simply isn't one of those people whose survival serves the common good. The very thought that one person might be less worthy of life than others demonstrates his ignorance of human rights, which in turn may serve to explain his limited value to a democratic society.

The patient leaves the house as seldom as possible, and every time he's forced to go out, he first checks to see if the coast is clear. The coast is seldom clear, hardly ever. The air usually isn't clean. When he gets a chalky taste in his mouth, he returns home. If he sees a bullet flash across the sky, he ducks into the nearest subway tunnel. More and more people are behaving in similar ways. Folie à deux: what two people was Celan referring to? The poet and the reader? Fear is a contagious illness known to every healthy person. The street is clean-shaven and swept bare. Some citizens have their own air-raid cellars, the cost of which they have no trouble deducting from their taxes. The patient isn't allowed to deduct the poetry books he buys as a professional expense. To begin with, he doesn't earn enough to be permitted to pay any income tax. Someday he'll earn a five-figure salary and deduct the medical reference book as a volume of poetry.

The patient can't get the verb *köpfeln* (to dive headfirst) out of his head; every three seconds the verb resounds at full volume and gives him no peace. The word would do better to remain in Celan's *detour garden,* having scarcely any application at all outside this poem. The patient's main error most likely consists of his constantly searching for the shortest route to the air-raid cellar instead of finding a poetic detour. A cellar can't be his home. A circus would offer better protection. That's a place the word *köpfeln* gets used, and any whales there aren't bombs: they are mammals that never drown. The patient suddenly resolves to go to Paris for the conference. It's his duty, his destiny, his first and final performance. There's an open newspaper lying on the table. He finds a tiny photograph of a whale diving into the water. Or maybe it's not an animal but a bomb? No, not that either. It's an airplane crashing. A suicide attack? No, an accident. A mechanical problem on a passenger flight en route to Paris. Most human problems are retroactively interpreted as mechanical problems. Among the bodies identified so far were seventeen Germans: two families finally taking a vacation after a long abstinence, a handful of businesspeople, and a young scholar on his way to a conference in Paris. In other words, my attempt to speak about *Threadsuns* was doomed even before my arrival at the conference. I hadn't considered this possibility. I was expecting to be torn to shreds *after* my talk. Someone would criticize my insufficient citations. Another person would list at least seventeen important aspects of the work I failed to address. A third would revile me as an anti-Semite, a fourth as an activist, while the fifth would be the worst: he would accuse me of stealing intellectual property since, apparently, a few years ago a young Chinese Germanist presented a quite similar theory. Later in Berlin he was beaten to death on the street by a right-wing extremist. I might even be accused of having incited this murder—or be forced to testify against my brother. Every breakdown of communication carries a paring knife in its breast pocket. What weapon can I use to defend myself? My hand grips a scalpel. Before I hurt someone with it, I'd best leap into the cold water to return to my senses. I become a whale and dive headfirst into the depths. What a shame, a journalist writes, this young academic had his whole career in front of him. My boss will tell everyone I've finally achieved my narcissistic goal of getting into all the major newspapers. My therapist will silently think to himself that when a plane crashes, it doesn't occur to anyone to suspect a suicide. But he killed himself before I did. He's no longer able to think anything at all. How can I sort out his death and my own chronologically?

All at once he succeeds: Patrik ascends from the deep ocean floor to the water's surface and beholds the sunlight. The time is 17:00 hours. He must have fallen asleep at some point. His body is bursting with the desire, as well as the strength, to undertake something. The musty bed insists on being left behind, the window aches to be flung open. A human being requires some impetus to take action, be it a gesture, a sign, or a word. Even a faint breath of wind is enough. The first poem is an inviting gesture, and to ignore it would be cowardly, spineless. Time to arise, collect oneself, and vertically enter the outside world! That's all the first voice in *Threadsuns* asks. Life can be as transparent as a poem. Arise and collect yourself! Am I truly awake, or am I just moving from the first act to the second in an ancient dream? Who's the conductor here? Who's the composer? *Who rules?* You have to be the ruler of your own life. This strikes the patient as all but impossible. Even as a child, he called his toy tractor "my colleague" and addressed his teddy bear as "Professor." His parents were delighted by their child's large vocabulary and unconcerned about his relationship to his belongings. The patient felt happy in the company of things, and it never occurred to him to seek mastery over them. These objects were alive, while living children were too unpredictable for him, too dangerous. Patrik, whose nickname was Pati, dreamed of going to school in another country, in Tibet for example, or in the Basque Country. The language there, he thought, would be completely different, and he wanted to learn it. As a little boy, Pati was shy and fearful. In adolescence, his face changed, and he appeared withdrawn but self-assured, while in reality he felt vulnerable, defenseless. The extensions of his veins fluttered freely in the air. Any time they got nicked, they would bleed. It was difficult to retract all these exposed nerves and lymph vessels back into his body. Pati manufactured a sort of protective clothing to cover these naked strands of soul. The clothing was made not of neoprene but of ordinary words. He draped the word *neck* around his neck like a scarf. For a glove, he tugged the four letters of the word *hand* over his fingers. *Shirt* and *pants* have five letters each, as does the *brain* he wore as a hat. *Hat, hair,* and *hand* all begin with *h*. These numbers and letters helped him, distracting him from his formless fear. He manipulated them into what eventually grew into a sort of private mysticism, which he deepened by reading widely in both dusty and freshly printed books that concerned themselves to a greater or lesser extent with mystics of yore. From Gershom Scholem he learned that Jewish mysticism can be understood as the product of crises. What Patrik sought was neither esoteric nor a conspiracy theory: he wanted something he described as mysticism. This is how he came to poetry.

After growing to full height and moving to Berlin, Patrik lost his wristwatch, refused to own a cell phone, and stopped eating meat. Private mysticism was a trap. This extreme fascination with letters of the alphabet and numbers sapped his libido. He took no interest in the sweet young creatures attempting to seduce him. His body was being occupied, overrun by letters that were tin soldiers firing hard figures at him. His *testes,* for example, which had six letters, fit neither in his *pants* nor his *brain,* where there was only room for five. He was forced to attend the institute with this body part exposed. His *buttocks,* of course, were far too big for a pair of five-letter *pants.* In a dream, he stood in front of City Hall, clean-shaven and neatly combed, but naked from the waist down.

Eventually he wanted to stop counting, to free himself from the cage of countable letters and go dancing every night. He wanted to excel at lightness and learn to say: "Oh, it really doesn't matter if there are only three letters, that's just how it is!" His therapist used to tell him that a person should be flexible. This banal piece of advice sounded like something he could put into practice. There was just one thing about it the patient found disconcerting: the word *flexible*—like *mobility* and *communication*—belonged to the vocabulary of people seeking and securing employment. A patient was not employable in any future. He did hold a part-time job at one point, but it was a dead-end position. There wasn't a single window in the corridor of the institute, and his office was a *standing-cell* with shelves crammed full of someone else's books. The bleak walls and pockmarked ceiling in the corridor were as coldly illuminated as a hospital ward, and when the head physician made his entrance, he spoke in such a baroque style that the fleeting thoughts of his meek-mannered assistant instantly became inaudible. The head physician wasn't a physician at all, he was a professor of German literature, but he liked to issue diagnoses nonetheless. He pronounced Celan a narcissist who had assumed all the critics would fall at his feet. When that failed to happen, the insulted poet unrolled the old rug stained with historical disgrace, thinking all his customers would rush to buy it—the same individuals responsible for causing the stains. Apparently, Celan couldn't tell the difference between trend and taboo and responded with overblown sensitivity to even the most innocuous displays of ignorance. He was in love with himself. Who but a narcissist would expect to be warmly embraced by the very people whose dirty, bloody scabs he had scratched open?

The head physician went on talking because no one could stop him. His condemnations grew harsher and ever more absurd. Celan, he proclaimed, lost his voice after *Breathturn*. He provoked the decent, well-educated citizenry by using terms and place names no one needs to know. *Pau,* for example! A person who goes around talking about *Pau* without a footnote is either impertinent or a foreigner.

Patrik didn't contradict his boss, but he secretly

resolved to study Celan's late poems. Pau isn't just a place Celan visited. P-a-u are the first three letters of the name Paul. This fact was overlooked by the famous Germanist who was Patrik's supervisor. One day Patrik would give a lecture in which he revealed the significance of every single letter Celan used in his poetry.

Another time, the chief physician cited Celan's love affairs as proof of his narcissism, above all the fact that he took his sexual escapades just as seriously as the psalms, those marvels of high culture. Spasms—I love you—psalms! What a narcissist a person must be to compare his own orgasm, his sperm, to the psalms! Patrik wanted to speak out against this exegesis dripping with scorn, but his voice failed him.

When the chief physician ran out of reprehensible remarks on the subject of Celan, he remarked that Stefan George had been a narcissist, as had Gottfried Benn and Georg Trakl. He rounded out his list of narcissists with the names of academic superstars, finally adding his own colleagues' names as well. You can always tell a narcissist by the way they go around accusing others of narcissism. Another clear characteristic of this disorder is the compulsion to ignore banal traffic rules. Patrik had heard this from his therapist, who sometimes told him jokes to lighten the mood. One of these was a joke Patrik remembered quite well: a narcissist in the snow. Through thickly falling snow a narcissist is driving 75 mph on the autobahn when he passes a sign that prohibits driving over 50 in snowy conditions. He doesn't slow down because he thinks the sign is for people who aren't good drivers. He even steps on the gas to make sure no one mistakes him for one of these average people. The therapist said that while this snow example sounds innocent, for an extreme narcissist, there's almost no difference between a traffic sign and Paragraph 211 of the German Criminal Code. If a narcissist finds it politically, morally, or economically expedient to commit a murder, he won't hesitate to kill.

It was early February. The chief physician was giving his assistant Patrik a ride from Hannover to Berlin. On the way, it began to snow. Patrik tried to remember which Celan poem contains a snowstorm. When the dreaded traffic sign came into view, his boss stepped on the gas. At the same time, he said that a person who has the nerve to strike out on his own as an author instead of supporting his family can only be egotistical and narcissistic. Patrik thought: Aha, maybe this distinguished professor wanted to be a poet when he was young. So his hatred was possibly just envy in disguise, directed exclusively at male poets. This was an error. His greatest hatred was reserved for a woman: Ingeborg Bachmann. Once, the chief physician was sitting with his doctoral students and faculty assistants at an Italian restaurant called The Eternal City. Patrik didn't want to join them but he hadn't managed to decline the invitation. The chief physician was talking about conferences in Rome and then out of the blue launched into a diagnosis of Bachmann. She had a personality disorder, he declared, and was utterly dysfunctional, which made her such a good fit for Celan. For the first time in his life, Patrik did something spontaneous. He asked an innocent question to avert an infinitely long hateful rant: What do you think of Nelly Sachs? The professor fixed a withering stare on this neophyte who obviously had no experience with women and replied: "Nelly Sachs isn't worth talking about since she was never a woman." Patrik stood up and brought his life as a research assistant to a close by walking out of The Eternal City. The *sandcastle* of his career crumbled soundlessly behind him.

6. *The Mummy Leap*

Off in the distance, someone is singing. It's a woman's voice, the tone quality is familiar, but the melody sounds different, in fact it's amazing Patrik can make out a melody at all. The voice hasn't soared to dizzying heights he would find overwhelming, it remains well within reach, it's just the language that evades his grasp. Where does one word end and another begin, maybe it's Czech. There's a sense of building and release in every note—even the eighth notes, possibly even the sixteenths. And so each tiny note forms a microcosm, one cosmos after another created and borne off on a great wave of breath into the future. There are no interruptions: even when a rest is indicated, you can still hear the sound of breathing.

The moon is the sole audience; it listens, inhaling every sound, growing rounder and rounder until it explodes in the night sky. Rusalka. The lunar shower of gold rains down on the singer's hair, her face is radiant, but a moment later it contorts in pain, perhaps because of the difficulty of producing notes. In a portrait, she can keep her lovely face, whereas onstage she's forced to surrender all static beauty and show this huge audience her naked, screaming musculature. A soprano's song is a cultivated scream. The singer masters the high art of controlling every strand of her vocal cords and therefore every fiber of her psyche. She can permit herself to scream from animalistic depths: the scream becomes music. She sings to the moon, for which there's no such thing as death. Patrik is only a shadow of this moon that can vanish at any moment—time need only beckon. He asks Dvořák to draw out the hour of the moon and, if possible, avoid landing on a final note. For as long as this song fills the night sky, Patrik can go on living. The moon slowly turns pale, and silence wakes the sleeper.

Patrik extracts himself from the sweaty bedsheets, pounces on his jacket, and starts digging through the pockets. The business card is still there, and the jacket has a human temperature, as if it had only just been removed from a body, though he may have spent several days tossing and turning sweatily in bed. His forehead is still damp, and when Patrik wipes it with the back of his hand, he feels a strange, unfamiliar skull underneath. His cheeks burn, his throat burns, and his lungs hang heavy as sandbags. He sits on the kitchen's lone chair. If he goes to see his doctor now, he might be sent to the hospital and held in isolation from the outside world for an unpredictable length of time. Before this happens, he definitely wants to have one more conversation with Leo-Eric to make sure the fresh flame of their friendship doesn't sputter out. Both times before, he was lucky and met his friend by chance at the café. This time he can't rely on chance alone. Patrik dials the number on the card. After two rings, a baritone answers.

"Chinese Cultural Institute. How may I help you?"

Patrik asks for Leo-Eric Fu. The response: a colorless silence. Patrik repeats the name and allows himself a joke:

"By the way, my favorite poet has the same last name: Du Fu."

"He's been dead for 1,300 years."

"Yes, I know. I'm not asking to speak to Du Fu, I'd like to speak with Leo-Eric Fu."

"No man by that name works here."

"That isn't possible. He gave me his business card."

"I'm sorry that I'm unable to help you."

It takes Patrik several seconds to realize the connection's been severed. His heart beats accelerando, crescendo, the entire apartment pounds and pounds with the beat. Until now, he's had no opportunity to confirm that this institute actually existed and that the number was correct. Now he knows the institute exists and he has the right number, but Leo-Eric doesn't work there. Or he works there and doesn't go by Leo-Eric, possibly because this name doesn't sound Chinese enough. It sounds more Jewish, French, or fictional. What part of this friendship is a fiction? Patrik pulls on his jacket, thrusts the business card deep in his pocket, and leaves the house. He turns right, breaking his ironclad rule to always turn to the left. Patrik descends into the inferno of the U-bahn station, which he hasn't set foot in for weeks. The train comes immediately, as if awaiting this moment. The conductor behind the glass looks like a shadow, his eyes impossible to discern. Maybe he's so tired he doesn't wish to be seen. The doors open automatically. Empty seats, dull windows covered with scratches, no smell of beer or perfume. At a new station that didn't exist before, he gets off. The Cultural Institute building is on an elegant street empty of people. The ornament above its grand portal looks playfully inviting, but the iron handle refuses to budge. A slip of paper has been taped above the tiny doorbell. It looks makeshift, unofficial, especially compared to the grand edifice housing the Institute. The slip of paper announces matter-of-factly that no cultural activities will be taking place until further notice.

Patrik decides to return to the U-bahn station, but when he turns around he can't believe his eyes. A slender man walks toward him: Leo-Eric. With his black suit, silk tie, and elegant leather shoes, he is dressed too formally for Berlin: one might get the impression he was on his way to a funeral.

"What are you doing here?"

Leo-Eric looks surprised and somewhat flustered, while Patrik's limbs quiver with joy. He extends his arms, shyly pulls them back again, then reaches out anew as if for an embrace that doesn't happen. Leo-Eric's eyelashes are laden with melancholy. He gives a few worried blinks, but his voice sounds cheerful as he proposes:

"There's a Tibetan snack bar nearby. Let's go there. My office work can wait."

Leo-Eric doesn't ask, for example, *why* Patrik is here. The two walk wordlessly side by side, making a right turn into a shady alleyway where they enter the little snack bar. At the table, Leo-Eric still doesn't ask his friend what's on his mind. His questions are confined exclusively to the menu. Patrik answers each question in the affirmative, without giving any thought to it, because life will now go on excellently with or without mushrooms. There was a time when he used specially cultivated mushrooms to combat his low moods. A Tibetan momo requires no hallucinogens to taste good. Deep fried or pan fried isn't such an important question either. The essential thing is for the friendship to remain delicious even after passing through the purgatory of the frying pan. Would Leo-Eric be eating at a Tibetan snack bar if he really were a diplomat working for the People's Republic? This, too, is a question that doesn't truly interest Patrik. At the moment, he's prepared to eat whatever shows up on his plate. His brain is in urgent need of fat, music shouldn't sound skimmed, and poetry too requires nutrients. He has no intention of singing with his own voice; he wants to talk about poems until his ears fill with music. That's the plan, and he's sure to succeed. Suddenly it occurs to him that he isn't at all prepared for this conversation.

"I'm so sorry, I don't have my book with me."

"What book do you mean?"

"The human body book you lent me."

"Keep it as long as you want. The more important question is whether you're hungry."

"I am! I had to perform hard physical labor today. In my dream."

"Who did you dream about?"

"A brutal hater of women. As a man, I'm actually in no danger, but I felt an uncontrollable fear, a *phosphorus fear*. I also dreamed of bombs falling from the sky."

The glass window frames a clear sky that Patrik perceives as more empty than blue. No bomb shadows anywhere in sight. A kitchen knife clomps rhythmically on the wooden board. Hot oil sizzles. Like two healthy young men, they sit across from each other at the small table. They will eat food that has been minced, kneaded, and fried, they will laugh often and say, "Oh yes."

"At our first meeting, you told me about the No-Tree," Patrik says. He's surprised he still remembers this tree, while Leo-Eric nods calmly, as if expecting this topic.

"Oh yes, that's my favorite tree. *No* is a soft word, despite being a negation. *No one* is a transparent person. *Never* will a time come that guarantees a more distant future. Do you know the poem 'NO SAND ART ANYMORE, no sand book, no masters'?"

"Oh yes, of course. It's from *Breathturn*. I don't intend to analyze *Breathturn*, but this book of poems marks the Copernican turn in Celan's poetry—without it there would be no *Threadsuns*."

"So you must also know the last lines of this poem. The letters are subtracted two at a time. At first you read: *Tief im Schnee*, 'Deep in snow,' though the three words are run together: *Tiefimschnee*. Then *t* and *sch* are removed. This produces a new word, *Iefimnee*. Then the e, *f*, *m*, *n*, and *e* disappear. All that's left in the end are three letters linked with hyphens: *I – i – e*. Do you know what the word *iie* means?"

"No."

"Precisely."

"Excuse me?"

"The word *iie* means 'no.'"

"In Chinese?"

"No, in Japanese. I know a Japanese woman in Paris whose father studied judo with Mikinosuke Kawaishi."

"Who is Miki . . . ?"

"The judo instructor of Moshé Feldenkrais."

"Aha, Feldenkrais," Patrik says. "Celan went to him for treatment."

"That's right, Franz Wurm made the referral. Kawaishi was famous for not using any Japanese numerals or concepts in his teaching. So the word *iie* couldn't have been passed to Celan from this judo master via Feldenkrais. But do you know what I think? A person who devotes his undivided attention to letters and numbers will sooner or later traverse the entire order of stars and organs. It wouldn't surprise me if Kabbalah intersected with acupuncture."

"I can easily imagine that," Patrik says. "What did Feldenkrais talk about with Celan? Was he able to help the despairing poet?"

"To help is hard, to cure even harder. Let's drop all these unrealistic expectations. Do you know what my Feldenkrais teacher did with me? He told me to interlace my fingers. When I do that, my right thumb automatically crosses over the left. Then he told me to interlace them the other way, left over right. It feels all wrong."

"What does that mean?"

"So many innocuous habits can reinforce a lopsided posture. I like to imagine Celan trying out something different with his hands. Naturally, Celan had real hands, too. Not just the hand as a word or metaphor."

Patrik remembers something his mother once told him: The way you cross your legs is genetically predetermined. But what about other habits? Is the fact that his parents never spoke about Ukraine also part of his genetic makeup? Leo-Eric interjects:

"Did you know that Moshé Feldenkrais came from Ukraine?"

The momo slips from Patrik's chopsticks, landing in his lap. How did Leo-Eric know Patrik's parents were Ukrainian?

"From where in Ukraine?"

With this question, Patrik indirectly confirms his connection to this country.

"Slavuta, I think. Feldenkrais didn't like talking about his childhood. He emigrated to Tel Aviv, and then Paris."

"To study judo?"

"No, judo was just his sideline. He was a physicist. He knew Marie Curie and other important researchers when radioactivity was first being artificially produced."

"You know a lot about him. Have you studied him?"

"No, but Masa—that's the name of my Japanese friend in Paris—told me a bit about him. Whenever we see each other, she talks like a waterfall about everything you can think of, and there are three people she especially likes talking about: her mother-in-law, Eugen Herrigel, and Moshé Feldenkrais. Masa says Feldenkrais was able to explain the techniques of judo from a scientific perspective, which went over well with his followers and made him famous in France."

"So he was both a physicist and a judo master—an interesting combination."

"For him, the teachings of judo were not at odds with scientific principles, but there were nonetheless moments that struck him as miraculous. I can remember one story Masa related to me. Once, Master Kawaishi lay on his back and asked two men to hold a long rod against his throat and press it firmly toward the ground on either side. To the onlookers' astonishment, the master easily slipped out from under the rod, as one might pull off a sweater."

Patrik is trying not to panic. For him, nothing is more terrifying than imagining his throat being crushed. Possibly this once happened to him in a distant past and he just can't remember.

A dense shadow darkens Leo-Eric's face, one that

wasn't there before. Patrik doesn't want to ask the reason for it. He hasn't been inhibited in his questions before, but this one question could put an abrupt end to the opera he's being allowed to sing in. He clings tightly to the topic of Feldenkrais so as not to have to speak about anything else.

"The childhood of a deer is so short it doesn't have time to acquire a bad posture. Human beings remain with their parents too long, and this leads to deformation, both mental and physical. I think Feldenkrais writes about this somewhere. If not, the idea is mine."

Leo-Eric laughs, temporarily relieving Patrik of the weight of the inexplicable shadow, and Patrik goes on talking.

"It's not that I believe that human beings are crueler than animals. A normal polar bear father doesn't recognize his children and will eat them if he's hungry. But Nature is intelligent and organizes the lives of bears in such a way that the children have single mothers who raise them."

"Feldenkrais wasn't as much of a pessimist as you. He even writes that there's no such thing as a wrong posture."

"Oh yes, that's right, it's coming back to me now. Our posture isn't wrong, it's just off-kilter in a different way for each of us. And we can work with that. A civilization-wide illness is a significant component of that civilization. Every feeling manifests itself in the musculature and leaves behind traces. That sounds a lot like Feldenkrais, doesn't it?"

"Certainly. That's why you can read personal memories in someone's musculature," Leo-Eric replies absentmindedly.

"But we aren't just bundles of nerves with reflexes, we're human beings who need a language—not just any language, a very particular one. This language can't cure us—it can even delay the healing process. Now and then we have to remove the language from the paper it's written on and take it back into our own hands. But what's the best way to do that?"

"That's something you should discuss with Celan, not me."

"Unfortunately he's been dead for half a century."

"Yes, but how can we be certain we aren't dead, too?"

Patrik looks in horror at his friend's face, not into his eyes but at the center of his forehead. Leo-Eric's face is gradually transforming into a round disk. Is it a clock, a DVD, a moon? The round face suddenly smiles, stretches back into its oval shape with black hair on top, and nods understandingly.

"I'll tell you a nice story. Masa once told me about a therapy she called Thread Mandala, or Thread Suns.

You're given a wooden hoop like the kind my mother used for embroidery. There are tiny numbered nails all around the rim. Without letting yourself be confused by the mysterious sequence of these numerals, you have to simply follow the colored threads of the prime numbers. Eventually you'll have a beautiful sun in your wooden frame. This therapy originated with Rudolf Steiner, and at some Waldorf schools it's still practiced in geometry class as a way to learn the prime numbers. Today, these thread suns are used in Japan to treat depression."

"Have you yourself ever seen a thread sun?"

"Yes, Masa showed me a gorgeous one that her daughter made: an incredible number of colorful threads crisscrossing to form a beautiful jagged pattern like a corona. When you look at the thread sun, all traces of gloom instantly vanish."

"Do you think Celan came into contact with this thread sun therapy, or maybe even tried it himself?"

"That seems highly unlikely. But spirits are constantly stretching colorful, multilingual threads above us, and we have no control over their activity."

Leo-Eric places his right hand upon the trembling left hand of his friend.

"I wasn't expecting to see you today, so our parting must take an unexpected form."

Leo-Eric takes out a sheet of paper from his briefcase. Patrik sees a rectangular burn mark and tiny, illegible writing. The burn mark might be a barcode. Patrik blinks frantically to avoid having to see Leo-Eric's crystalline eyes. They are bewitching, but inhuman. His voice arrives from some far-distant location that Patrik is powerless to pinpoint.

"This is a copy of your e-ticket for Paris. You're registered for the conference. You've already started your flight. You can read in the newspaper what happened. Maybe you saw the newspaper I left on your desk. Time can't be turned back—it twists in on itself, and during one of these twistings we experience a parting that in reality never happened."

Patrik drains the dregs of his water glass, stands up, and climbs onto the back of his friend, who has knelt on the ground and spread his wings. The bird body is as soft as a down comforter—not particularly warm, but still he finds it pleasurable to close his eyes, release his thoughts, and let himself be borne aloft. Patrik has completed his part of the score, now he's allowed to stop sorting out letters and numbers and also to stop attempting to sing, for in the space of time he's now entering, there is no such thing as music.

Afterword

Yoko Tawada's novel, written in Berlin during the first year of the COVID-19 pandemic, pays homage to Paul Celan, a longstanding influence on her work. Arguably the most important German-language poet of the post-World War II era, Celan is known for the diamond-hard density of his lyrical lines, his technique of compounding and compacting language into often surprising portmanteau images, estranging words from their inherited meanings, and thereby opening up new avenues of association and interpretation.

Celan's poetry is also suffused with the trauma of having lived through the Holocaust. He was born in Czernowitz, a famously multicultural, polyglot city located then in Romania and now in Ukraine. During the Second World War, Czernowitz was occupied first by the Soviets—in 1941, when Celan was twenty—then by German and Romanian troops who established a ghetto that confined the city's Jewish residents. Celan's parents were deported from Czernowitz in 1942 to a labor camp where both died soon thereafter: his father, Leo, of typhus, his mother shot and killed by a guard. Celan, who spent much of the war years imprisoned in a labor camp as well, emerged traumatized and in mourning. Though he wrote almost all his poetry in German, Celan moved to Paris in 1948 and remained there for the rest of his life, marrying the artist Gisèle Lestrange and fathering a son, Eric.

In *Paul Celan and the Trans-Tibetan Angel,* the protagonist—a (former?) research assistant at the (fictional) Institute for World Literature in Berlin—deliberates whether or not to attend a Paul Celan conference in Paris. He does a lot of quoting from his favorite poet in his conversations with the "Trans-Tibetan" man he meets one day at a café, Leo-Eric Fu. (The word "Trans-Tibetan" comes from Celan's poem "WHEN I DON'T KNOW, DON'T KNOW.") In my translation of Tawada's novel, I quote whenever possible from Pierre Joris's translations of Paul Celan's poems, in particular the volume *Breathturn into Timestead,* published in 2014 by Farrar, Straus and Giroux—though I do sometimes depart from this translation whenever Tawada's readings of the lines diverge from those of Joris, as is inevitable with Celan. Note that the convention of printing part or all of the first lines of untitled poems in small caps is Celan's own.

Catching every last reference to Celan's work is not at all essential for enjoying and understanding this novel, but the reader should be aware that surreptitious, unidentified Celan quotes can be found on many of its pages. Tawada has constructed a world that embodies the protagonist's Celanian desires, and his thoughts and observations are frequently laced with phrases and words from Celan's poems. Rolling the dice, Van Gogh's severed ear, the krater, foam, needles, hammers, pomegranate, quince, lips, blackbird, jackdaw, cockchafer, diving whales, phosphorus, comets, corona, melancholy, hard silence, and folie à deux are all borrowings from Celan's poetic universe, and this list is by no means exhaustive.

My favorite Celan reference in the novel appears when Leo-Eric describes the "No-Tree" that gives a different answer to every question posed to it, although the answer is always "No." While this tree reminds the protagonist of a Zen Buddhist koan, it reminds *me* of these lines from Celan:

Die Krücke im Tal,
von Erdklumpen umschwirrt,
von Geröll, von
Augensamen,
blättert im hoch
oben erblühenden Nein—in der
Krone.

The crutch in the valley,
whirred about by earthclods,
by gravel, by
eyeseed,
leafs through the high-
up flowering No—in the
crown.

These Celan (and Joris) lines from the poem "DIE WAHRHEIT, angeseilt an ..." (TRUTH, roped to ...) show Celan at his most extreme Hölderlin-influenced syntactical complexity. The "truth" presented in this poem is told slant (Celan was a devoted translator of Emily Dickinson), and through these lines that gesture at description instead of naming outright, the image of a tree emerges. Planted in a valley, a crutch grows into a tree in whose crown a "No" blossoms. And by a slantwise process of association, this image also blossoms into the No-Tree in Tawada's novel.

Slantwise association is also the principle linking the forms of trauma explored in the book with other sources of distress the reader will no doubt recognize: the global COVID-19 pandemic as well as the suffering caused by toxic masculinity, racism, xenophobic hate, capitalism's insatiable demands, and the constant assaults on the very notion of truth by authoritarian "poplarists," to use Tawada's playful, arboreal epithet.

For all the lighthearted inventiveness with which Tawada takes on these subjects, a deep thread of melancholy runs through the book as well.

Yet Tawada's novel—like Celan's poetry—constantly returns to the notion of connection. She writes of the solace of friendship, conversation, reading, music, of seeing and being seen. These are the meridians weaving her book together across decades, languages, and cultures.

— SUSAN BERNOFSKY

NEW YORK, DECEMBER 2023

Acknowledgments

For crucial assistance, the translator would like to thank Amanda Hong, Richard Gehr, and the book's editor, Jeffrey Yang, as well as Pierre Joris for his inspiring decades-long devotion to the work of Paul Celan.

YOKO TAWADA was born in Tokyo in 1960, moved to Hamburg when she was twenty-two, and moved again to Berlin in 2006. She writes in both Japanese and German, and has published dozens of books—stories, novels, poems, plays, essays—in each language. She has received numerous awards for her writing including the Akutagawa Prize, the Adelbert von Chamisso Prize, the Tanizaki Prize, the Kleist Prize, and the Goethe Medal. New Directions publishes nine of her books, including *The Emissary,* which won the inaugural National Book Award for Translated Literature in 2018.

SUSAN BERNOFSKY has translated more than twenty books, including, for New Directions, Yoko Tawada's *Where Europe Begins, The Naked Eye,* and *Memoirs of a Polar Bear* (winner of the Warwick Prize for Women in Translation); six titles by Robert Walser; and five by Jenny Erpenbeck, including *The End of Days* (winner of the Independent Foreign Fiction Prize). She is the author of *Clairvoyant of the Small: The Life of Robert Walser,* and teaches at Columbia University, where she also directs the literary translation program.